Alayna~
Enjoy!
BB Swann

BREAKING
THE
BRO CODE

A Breakin in the 80s Novel

CHAPTER ONE

MOLLY

Torture had never been her thing, but Molly Mason endured it walking with her boyfriend Trevor through the mall. She glanced at his profile and stifled a sigh. He loved it. The noise, the crowds, the stares directed at them from other girls, jealous that he chose her over them. He smiled at them because as a theater guy, the attention suited him. She, however, preferred a quiet trail with her feet propelling her forward—toward a better future.

"Let's go into Spencer's." Trevor pulled her by the hand, cutting across the stream of people walking along the shiny, white tiled floor. "I love this store."

"I don't," Molly mumbled, but he continued to guide her until they had entered the cluttered gag gift shop.

Trevor released her hand. He weaved through the narrow aisles and headed for the back of the store. A tall red head smiled at him and he smiled back, nodding politely. Molly smirked at the disappointed look the girl gave Trevor, amazed again that he had chosen to date her when he had so many other choices.

Not that she was ugly. Hours spent training had given her a fit body, even if it was only five feet tall. And Trevor always complimented her long blonde hair and silvery gray eyes. Still, comparing herself to some of the girls who flirted with Trevor made her throat tight.

She followed Trevor through the store with a frown. His intended destination *always* made her frown. "Trevor, why do you look at this stuff. It's totally gross."

He snorted a breath out his nose. "To you. I think it's funny." Reaching for a shelf, he grabbed a package and grinned. "See, like this. Can you imagine the look on your mom's face if she saw this in your room?"

Molly glared at the clear plastic bag filled with extra-large, glitter-infused ribbed condoms. She snatched it and tossed it back onto the shelf. "Very funny. Especially considering we don't do that, and I would never use something like this if we did."

Trevor wrapped his arms around her waist and pulled her closer. "C'mon, Molly. You know I'm just joking."

He leaned in to kiss her and his soft lips melted away her irritation. Molly kissed him back for a moment then laid her head on his chest.

"Of course," he said, "I am open to trying something new." He slid his hands to her butt and squeezed.

"Trev," she grabbed his hands and stepped back with a nervous laugh. "I'm… uh…going to go check out the t-shirts."

He pressed his lips together for a second. "Ok."

He turned back to the wall, and Molly walked toward the front of the store and the less suggestive items. She stopped at a rack crammed with band t-shirts.

Why was everything about sex? Every movie, every song, every conversation at the parties she and Trevor went to on the weekends. She shook her head and searched through the overloaded display. Pawing aside the wrinkled shirts, she bit her bottom lip.

Not that sex would be a bad thing with Trevor. He was hot for sure. His tall, well-built body, Brett Michaels hair and those gorgeous lips made her stomach tingle every time he touched her.

For whatever reason though, Molly just couldn't do it. Something didn't feel right, like there was some spark or magic missing and every time they came close, she chickened out.

Slamming the hangers aside, Molly pursed her lips. Maybe she was a prude, this was the eighties, and at seventeen, she could make her own decisions. She glanced up, searching for Trevor and caught a glimpse of the back of his head as he moved to another area of the shop. His shoulder length blond hair glimmered under the flashing neon lights from the signs for sale on the walls.

Yep, totally righteous, just not exactly... right. For now.

She watched him for another moment. He laughed with the girl standing next to him. Another one of his traits; he could talk to anyone. No shyness like Molly.

Smiling, Molly returned her attention to the rack and paused on a white shirt with black three-quarter length sleeves. On the front, a thin blue circle house a screen print of Bon Jovi, one of her favorite bands. The rockers, with their big hair and leather clad legs, each gave a one-armed fist pump in typical rocker style.

"Yes! Finally." Molly pushed her hands into the fabric sea and yanked the shirt from the rack. Closing her eyes, memories of the concert she and her best friend, Cindy, had gone to, flooded her mind. The screaming, the blaring guitars, John Bon Jovi dancing on the stage in his tight pants. She shivered, humming the tune to Shot Through the Heart. The concert had been a for Cindy's birthday, courtesy of her friend's parents. A rare treat for Molly considering she and her mom were lucky to have any extra money for buying pop-tarts let alone a concert ticket.

Getting a shirt at the outrageous prices the vendors wanted was out of the question. So, Molly had searched the stores afterward, but they'd sold out fast. Her heart soared at the chance to get one. Running her fingers along the sleeve, she found and raised the price tag.

Her flipping stomach slammed to a dead stop as she stared at the number.

"Darn it." She clutched the shirt with shaky fingers then returned it to the rack.

"Hey." Trevor hugged her from behind, pointing to the shirt. "Isn't that the concert you and Cindy went to?"

"Yeah." She gazed at the picture.

"You gonna get it?"

"No. It… It's not my size."

Trevor grabbed the shirt and held it up to Molly. "Looks like it will fit."

"That's okay. I don't need it."

She took a step toward the door, but he grabbed her arm. "What's the matter?"

"Nothing. C'mon, let's just go." With a lawyer for a dad, Trevor didn't understand Molly's need to be frugal. It was easier not talk to him about her lack of money.

"You are such a terrible liar. Is it the money?"

Heat filled her face. "No."

Trevor held her hand and led her to the counter. He handed the shirt to the cashier.

"You don't have to buy it. Really. I don't want—"

"Yes, you do want it. And it's no big deal. I'll get it for you."

"That's okay. Don't waste your money."

He handed a twenty to the guy behind the counter. "It's not that much. Besides, you can pay me back later if it makes you feel better."

Tears filled Molly's eyes. "You're too good to me."

"Anything for my girl." Trevor kissed her cheek and handed her the bag. They left the store and re-joined the throng of shoppers. After traveling past the indoor merry-go-round crawling with screaming kids, he pulled her into an alcove next to a metal gated store front with a large coming soon sign hung from the top. The sound of hammers and drills drifted from inside the construction site.

"What are we—"

"I think I'll take a bit of that payment now." Smiling, he backed her against the wall then, holding her cheeks, he pressed his lips to hers.

Molly hugged his neck and returned his kiss, her chest filled with heat. Was that the spark she needed? Teasing moments like this made her want to give him everything he asked for. His playful smiles, his tender kisses, the way he made her feel so loved. Guilt twisted in her gut knowing she always let him down.

Trevor slid his hands to her waist and moved even closer, slipping his tongue into her mouth and pushing against her with his hips. His quick breaths fanned her face and he put one hand behind her neck, holding her tight.

"Trevor…" She put her hands on his chest.

"You want to get out of here?" he asked, trailing kisses along her cheeks and to her neck.

Molly's muscles tightened in her back. Fear doused the spark like dipping a match in water. "Uh, well. I thought we were... going to eat lunch."

"Is that what you really want right now?" He chuckled. "Because I can think of something better than food."

He kissed her again before she could answer, but she pushed against his chest and he stopped.

"I'm sorry," Molly said.

He narrowed his blue eyes for a second, then closed them, leaning his forehead against hers. "Yeah. I know. Let's go eat."

Molly sighed then took his hand in hers. "Can we stop by the bathroom first?"

Stepping backward, Trevor pulled her with him and re-joined the throng in the main walkway. "Anything for my girl."

Molly gave him a sideways glance. Her heart skipped a beat at the frown on his face and the guilt punched her in the stomach.

Yep, letting him down again.

They reached the hall leading to the bathroom and Trevor stopped, glancing around them at the shoppers. "I'll wait out here."

"Okay." Molly squeezed his hand and rushed down the hall. Fighting back tears, she pushed the door open and went inside the bathroom.

A few minutes later, after drying her hands on a paper towel, Molly opened the door and tossed the paper in the trash by the door. She walked through the hall, looking for Trevor—and jerked to a stop.

Trevor stood with his back against the brick wall under a sign that read *Restrooms*, a brilliant smile on his face. But it wasn't for Molly. Another girl stood with him, playing with the edges of his jean jacket. Andrea, a girl from their school—the one Molly consistently beat in every cross-country race. She said something to Trevor, and he laughed touching the tip of her nose with his fingertip.

Heat scorched Molly's face and chest. She narrowed her eyes and stalked over to them. Trevor looked up as she approached and raised his eyebrows for a second. Then he pushed off the wall and reached for Molly.

"Hey." He gestured to Andrea. "Look who I ran into."

Molly met Andrea's gaze and nodded. "Hi, Andrea."

Andrea cocked her eyebrow, flipping her long brown hair over her shoulder and looked at Trevor. "I'll see you later." She glanced at Molly and grinned, then walked away through the crowd.

Biting her tongue, Molly glared at Trevor. "What the hell?"

A wrinkle formed between his eyes. "What?"

"What do you mean what? What was that all about?" She waved a hand in the direction Andrea had walked.

"Jeez, relax. We were just talking." He took her hand in his and pulled her toward the food court.

Molly yanked her hand away and planted her feet. "No, you were flirting with her."

"I was not flirting." He narrowed his eyes. "You're overreacting."

"She had her hands all over you and you touched her. That's not *just talking*." Molly clenched her hands into fists to stop them from shaking.

Trevor huffed a breath. "Great. You think I'd do that? Nice."

"What am I supposed to think?"

"You're supposed to trust me." He pushed out his bottom lip. "I guess I haven't earned that from you."

Molly stared at him, her mouth opened slightly, and eyebrows drawn into a deep V. She remembered the way he smiled at the other girls today and considered that in the light of this new information. Her stomach clenched.

"You've been smiling at other girls all day and I thought you were just being friendly. But it's more than that, isn't it?"

"No." He crossed his arms. "Look, you know I think you're beautiful, but it's human nature to look at people. You aren't the most beautiful girl out there just like I'm not the cutest guy. You look at other guys, too, and I never give you a hard time."

Molly gasped. "I do not." How had this turned into *her* fault?

"I've seen it. And you talk to them, too. But I trust you, so I don't let it bother me."

"I... I haven't." But that wasn't true. She talked to the guys on the cross team. And Hayden, Trevor's best friend. Did Trevor think she was flirting, too?

Trevor drew a deep breath and dropped his gaze to the floor. He raised his eyes and tears glimmered on his lashes. "I love you, Molly. But how can we move forward if you don't trust me?"

Molly caught her breath, her heart pounding against her ribs. She sighed and took his hands in hers. "It just looked like you were enjoying her attention."

"I didn't want to hurt her feelings." He pulled Molly to his chest and wrapped his arms around her waist. "Please, don't worry about her. She's not the one I want."

Laying her cheek against his soft shirt, Molly hugged his waist, too. "I guess I was just jealous. Sorry." Let down number ten thousand.

His laugh rumbled under her ear. "That's okay. I'd feel the same way if I saw you with another guy." He lifted her chin with a finger and kissed her softly on the lips.

Molly relaxed into him for a moment then smiled. "Alright, now that the drama is over, let's eat."

"You got it. Anything for my girl." He caressed her cheek with his fingertips and smiled,

Molly did too and turned toward the circle of food counters and tables. As they walked, she sighed, pushing Andrea and any residual hurt from her mind. Trevor loved her, and that was all that mattered.

Besides, I'll take care of Andrea myself tomorrow.

CHAPTER TWO

MOLLY

Molly bolted through the trees, the raspy breaths of her pursuers driving her forward. The smell of muddy, rotten leaves drifted on a breeze too weak to dry the sweat trickling into her eyes. She didn't dare take the time to wipe it away. She pushed her feet faster, legs pumping, arms swinging. Her rapid, beating heart, throbbing inside her chest.

The trees reached toward her, half empty branches like the claws of gigantic, mangy, orange and red cats. She pounded her feet through dirt littered with clumps of color from their autumn coats. She dodged a fallen, ankle-breaking branch, hoping it didn't slow her too much.

She couldn't let them catch her. She wouldn't. She never had before. Gritting her teeth, she glared at the oncoming hill and sucked in a deep breath, her lungs burning, pulling strength from inside her core to power her way to the top.

She broke from the trees and onto the dew-filled grass of the hill.

"Push it, Molly! Faster!" Trevor's voice pulled her toward the finish line, toward victory.

"Go, Molly! You got this!" Hayden's voice joined Trevor's, adding to the adrenaline coursing through her blood.

Molly didn't even look at them, she focused on the tape. The girls behind her would do the same, but they wouldn't pass her now. Not when she'd worked this hard.

Step. Breathe. Step. Breathe. She increased the rhythm. Faster and faster, until her lungs screamed, her muscles burned. Almost there. Just a little further. The crack of a stick told her someone crept up from behind.

"No." The breathless grunt escaped, and Molly used the word to fuel her last few steps. The thundering sound of that little word eclipsed the cheers of the crowd, the screams of her coach, even Trevor and Hayden's voices.

Molly blasted across the finish line, her chest breaking the tape. Now she slowed, her feet slapping the ground, arms relaxing from their bent position, lungs pulling in deep breaths of the cool morning air. She smiled at her new personal record time flashing on the clock.

She clasped her hands behind her head to catch her breath. Her nearest pursuer followed in three seconds and Molly turned to congratulate her. The greeting stuttered off her lips when she saw who it was; Andrea, one year younger than Molly and Hayden's latest reject.

"Good job." Remembering the mall, the smile Molly tried for didn't even reach her lips.

Andrea glared back, her lip curling at the corner. "Yeah, you too. NOT." She stomped away, her dark brown ponytail bouncing back and forth with her steps.

Molly muttered under her breath. "Sore loser."

She ignored Andrea and paced, watching the other top runners cross the line. Once her breathing slowed to a more normal rhythm, she, ducked under the roped off corral, and walked away from the finish area. She went where Trevor waited behind the crowd, hugging him around the neck.

He kissed her then smiled. "Congratulations."

She stepped back to thank him. Before she could speak, Hayden grabbed her from behind and swung her around by her waist.

She laughed. "Put me down you idiot."

Hayden laughed, too, then squeezed her in a bear hug. "Great race. Nice kick at the end. You should have seen Andrea's face when you beat her... a-gain."

Molly grinned. "Well, I haven't lost to her yet. And I couldn't let it happen today with the scouts here." A scholarship was her only way out of this craptastic small town, and she wasn't letting anything, or anyone, stop her from getting it.

Hayden looked at the stands. "Where are they?"

She shrugged. "I don't know. They're probably with the coach."

"I'll bet they're impressed. You had a great race today." Hayden winked, his bright green eyes twinkling in the sun.

Molly chuckled then glanced at Trevor. Her stomach dropped. "Is something wrong?" She touched his arm and his frown disappeared.

Trevor shook his head. "Nothing's wrong." He shifted his gaze to Hayden, narrowing his eyes slightly. "Dude, you need to leave."

Molly frowned, glancing between them. Trevor's lip twitched and her stomach tensed. Hayden acted the same at every race, but it never caused a problem before.

But Hayden laughed then smiled at her. "Gotta jet. Practice starts in ten minutes."

Trevor snorted. "You're so busted."

Sighing, she looked at Hayden's cleats and shin guards and shook her head. "You won't make it. You should have left sooner."

He brushed his hand through his spiky dark hair. "Right. I'm the captain, what's Coach going to do, bench me?"

"Whatever just go." She pushed his chest. "Thanks for coming to cheer me on."

Hayden's gaze lingered on her for a moment and Molly's breath caught in her throat. Trevor slid his arm around her, and she jumped.

A hint of a crease appeared between Hayden's eyes then he smiled at her. "Anytime." He nodded to Trevor then turned and jogged toward the parking lot.

Trevor pulled her closer and pressed his lips to hers with a soft kiss. "Good race but it got a little close at the end. Were you distracted by something?" He tucked a loose strand of hair behind her ear.

Her back stiffened at the criticism. "No, some races are better than others." Did he not even realize she had run her best time of the year?

Trevor glanced at Hayden's retreating back and the frown returned. "Maybe too many eyes were watching."

"If I can't focus because people are watching then I don't have a hope of getting a scholarship." She tapped his nose with her finger. "I like it when you guys come to watch. Don't worry though while I'm running, I don't even know you're there."

Trevor squinted. "Gee, thanks. Glad to see how important I am."

She grabbed his hands, her stomach tightening again. "That's not what I meant. I..."

Trevor squeezed her hands. "I know what you meant. Don't worry about it."

She held her breath for a second. "Is something else bothering you? Are you still upset about yesterday?"

He sighed. "I don't…"

Another set of arms wrapped her in a hug from behind. "Girrll! Please, tell me you won. I couldn't stand it if that skanky ho beat you."

Trevor rolled his eyes.

Molly giggled and turned to hug her best friend, Cindy. "You know I did. Andrea was gracious about it, too."

Cindy threw her head back and laughed. Her springy black curls bobbed in her loose ponytail.

Trevor took a step back, frowning at Cindy.

"Hey, Trevor." Cindy flipped her hair back.

"What's up Cindy? You finished." He smirked. "Better than the last meet, I hope. Aren't you supposed to be faster?"

Molly sighed, sure the insults were about to fly. She wished her best friend and boyfriend could like each other.

Cindy raised her eyebrows and put her hands on her hips. "Why? Because I'm black?"

Molly held back a laugh at the shocked look on Trevor's face.

"Uhh… no. Because you're fast on the track." He glanced at Molly and raised an eyebrow.

She giggled, rubbing her hand along his arm. "Sprinting and long distance are two different races. Runners aren't always good at both."

Cindy snorted. "Except for you, girl." She nodded at someone behind Molly. "You better go to coach Davis. She's looking this way."

Two men stood next to their coach. The college logos on their shirts sent her heart racing again. She waved to the coach.

"I gotta go. Wish me luck, Trev." She touched his cheek. Her breath hitched at his glare.

"Right, well, enjoy your fan club. Good luck." He walked away shaking his head.

Cindy growled under her breath. "Ignore him. He's being his normal dickhead self. Go talk to the coaches. You've earned it. Let's hang out after and you can give me the 411."

Molly nodded at her best friend but gazed after Trevor remembering their fight at the mall. *Dammit, I did it again.* She swallowed hard, then returned her gaze to Cindy's wide eyes.

"Okay. Wait here and we can go eat." Molly lifted her chin and walked toward the coaches, toward her future, toward freedom.

CHAPTER THREE

HAYDEN

Coach Jones frowned. "You're late."

Hayden threw his bag on the sideline. "Sorry, Coach. It won't happen again."

The coach nodded and pointed to the others. Hayden joined his teammates warming up on the field.

Tim, Andrea's brother, greeted him with a salute. "Nice of you to show up, Captain."

"I'm only a couple minutes late. Went to the meet." Hayden grabbed a ball from the practice bag. Tim stepped back, and Hayden passed to him.

Trapping the ball with his foot. Tim glared. "So, did you see my sister run? How'd she do?"

"Got second." He gestured to his foot and Tim passed the ball back with pace. Hayden raised an eyebrow and chuckled to himself. Dating Tim's sister had been a bad idea. They'd only gone on one date but she for sure wasn't his type; bitchy, conceited, and a little mean. Kind of like Tim.

"I'm sure Molly won again. Andrea hates her." Tim shook his head. "I don't know what Trevor sees in her. She's weird."

Hayden gritted his teeth and slammed his foot into the ball. It flew, hitting Tim in the chest. "Sorry. Kicked it too hard."

He jogged back a few steps waiting for the return pass. They continued to warm up in silence. Tim's passes got progressively harder and Hayden returned each with a grin.

Coach blew his whistle. "Let's go ladies. Time to work on finishing."

Hayden jogged toward the box, the others falling in behind him, like always. Frowning, he mumbled under his breath. "Quack, Quack." Even Tim deferred to him when it came to soccer.

"Alright. Cross and finish. Hayden, Tim, you're up." The coach took his spot on the edge of the box to watch the drill.

Hayden led off, passing the ball to Tim on the outside corner. He crossed the ball back but instead of hitting Hayden's feet, Tim blasted the ball up high. Hayden avoided taking a blow to the face and headed it into the goal.

He glared at Tim. Asshole. Yep, dating Tim's sister was the worst idea ever. She wasn't the one he wanted to be with.

Coach called to them. "Great finish, Hayden. But, Tim, you're supposed to play his feet."

Tim grinned. "Sorry. Kicked it too hard." His red hair and matching freckles blazed in the afternoon sunshine, just like his temper.

Hayden laughed on his way back to the line. Sometimes Tim could be funny.

When practice ended, Hayden sat on the bench to change out of his cleats. He rubbed his chest where Tim's last pass had hit. "Damn." He winced and shook his head.

His friend Mike, the goalie, fell into the seat beside him. "Tim's pissed at you. I told you his sister wasn't worth it." Mike stripped off his cleats.

Hayden snorted. "Yeah, I should've listened to you." He threw his shoes into his soccer bag. "She's a bitch. Not worth having Tim mad at me. Especially if he's going to take it out on me with a soccer ball."

He leaned back and sighed, another face entering his mind.

"Besides, I know who you're looking at." Mike slid on his tennis shoes. "And I'm here to tell you that's a bad idea, too."

Hayden wrinkled his eyebrows. "What are you talking about?"

"You know exactly what I'm talking about. She's off-limits to you."

Hayden clenched his jaw. "I'm not looking at anybody." He'd been keeping his feelings for her secret long enough the lie glided off his tongue.

"So, if Molly walked up right now and jumped in your lap you wouldn't get a boner and try to kiss her?" Mike pulled on his sweatshirt, flattening his blond spikes. He ran a hand over his head to fix them.

Hayden twitched his fists. "You're crazy. She's my best friend's girlfriend." *Shit, am I that obvious?*

Mike frowned. "And that's why she's off-limits. You have to honor the bro code man." He stood and grabbed his bag. "I'm looking out for you, Hayden. Trust me. You don't want to lose a friend over a girl, no matter how smokin' she is."

"Whatever, dude. Molly's not my type." He dug in his bag, avoiding Mike's knowing eyes.

Mike slapped him on the shoulder. "Sure. I've got to go. See ya later."

Hayden stayed on the sun-warmed bench watching the cars leave the parking lot. He leaned forward. Resting his elbows on his knees, he held his head in his hands. Mike was right. Molly was off-limits.

But she wasn't just *a* girl, she was *the* girl.

He rubbed his face and stood from the bench thinking back to when he'd first met Molly during track last year. He loved her shy smile, and her gorgeous body definitely excited him, but her skill on the track impressed him even more. She was the fastest on the girl's team. Faster even than some of the guys on Hayden's.

He sighed. "I should have asked her out then."

At the time, introducing her to Trevor had seemed like a good idea. She was new and didn't know many people. He'd wanted to make her feel comfortable.

Hayden grabbed his bag and headed toward his car, remembering the worst day of his life.

He and Trevor had been at the arcade after track practice, back when they still used to hang out. The beeps and whistles of the games had competed with the voices and laughter and the occasional squeals of the patrons. Pet Shop Boys blared on the speakers, echoing through the pizza and popcorn scented room.

Molly had been there, too, with Cindy. He'd introduced her to Trevor, and they'd all talked until Cindy pulled her away to play games. Hayden had waited for a chance to talk to her again, sneaking glances, waiting for Cindy to leave her alone.

Trevor stood next to Hayden leaning against the Pac Man machine while Hayden played. He glanced at Molly, too. "She's hot. Think she'd go out with me?"

"I don't know." Hayden jammed the joystick side to side. He watched her playing Donkey Kong, laughing at something Cindy said. Hayden smiled, too.

Trevor nudged him with his elbow. "You want to ask her out, don't you?"

Yes. He didn't want to be obvious, so he shrugged. "I don't know."

"Well, I do. I'm going for it." Trevor pushed off the machine and strode toward Molly just as Cindy walked away.

And Hayden had watched Trevor take the girl he wanted, turning Hayden's life into a stupid Rick Springfield song.

Hayden reached his car and threw his bag in the trunk, slamming the lid. He sat in the driver's seat, leaning his head back on the headrest.

"I'm such a dumbass." He started his car and put in his Cure cassette. *Boys Don't Cry* came on and Hayden smirked.

"Perfect."

He hit fast forward. *Jumping on Someone Else's Train* sounded like less drama.

On the drive home, he tried to convince himself Molly was off-limits. But then he remembered hugging her today, remembered her hand pushing on his chest. Every time she slapped his arm or shoved his shoulder, his heart raced, and a smile slipped out.

That was, until Trevor entered the vision and slid his hands onto her. Hayden gripped the steering wheel. "Damn it. Forget it. Mike's right. You can't break the bro code."

He turned the corner and pulled into his driveway, nodding to himself. Right. Off-limits. Find someone else.

Hayden grimaced. It was impossible to lie to himself.

CHAPTER FOUR

MOLLY

Molly slid into Cindy's blue Ford Escort and closed the door, smiling.

Cindy clapped her hands and bounced in the driver's seat. "Well, what did they say? What did they offer? Are you going to UCLA or Arizona? Was U of I there? Do they want you, too? Come on, spill, spill!"

Molly laughed. She waited, teasing a little longer. "I didn't get an official offer yet from anyone. But, UCLA and U of I will be at sectionals next week to see how I do. They said I have a promising future." Cindy's squeal echoed through the car and Molly covered her ears.

She grabbed Molly's hands and bounced even harder in the seat. "Omigod, omigod! This is so exciting!"

Molly laughed. When Cindy broke into valley girl, it meant she was serious. "I know. But now I'm super nervous about next week. What if I screw up? What if Andrea beats me?" She leaned back on the seat and groaned. "What if I crack under the pressure?"

"I won't let you." Cindy smiled at her. "Come on, let's get your mind off it with food. I'm starving. Where should we go?"

Molly's stomach grumbled. "I don't have much cash. Let's go to Taco Bell. Then we can feed the games some quarters at the arcade next door and re-live our younger years."

"Sounds good." Cindy started her car then sped away from the cross-country course.

They passed the soccer fields and Molly looked out the window. She smiled at Hayden dribbling the ball down the field, glancing back when Cindy cleared her throat.

Cindy rolled her eyes. "So, are you and Trevor going out tonight? Or can we have a girl's night instead?"

Molly turned back to watch Hayden while they continued past the fields. Cindy turned a corner, and he disappeared from her view. She bit her bottom lip. "I don't know. I think he's mad at me again. I'll have to call you and let you know."

"Girl, you know how I feel about Trevor. Yeah, he's cute with that rocker hair. But good looks don't matter when the personality is ugly." Cindy frowned. "He treats you bad."

Molly shook her head. "No, he doesn't. I think he's just insecure."

Cindy parked in the Taco Bell lot and cut the engine. "If he doesn't trust you, he's the one with the problem. Having four brothers makes me somewhat of an expert on boy's behavior. I know how men should treat a lady. Trevor never got the memo. I'd never put up with that shit from a guy, no girl should."

"You don't know him like I do. When it's just us he's super sweet." Molly smiled. "And he's a great kisser."

"Hmm hmmm. But sex is no reason to stay with a man." Cindy got out of the car.

Molly followed, her face hot. "I'm not talking about sex."

"He still pressuring you?" Cindy's eyes narrowed. She walked through the door and they got in line. "You know he ain't the one."

"How do you know? Maybe he is." Molly looked at the floor, avoiding Cindy's steady stare. "He says he loves me."

"I love you too, but you don't hear me pressuring you to do something that could damage your future."

Molly laughed. "I know. But he's disappointed every time I say no. He's my boyfriend and I want him to be happy." Was it such a big deal if she did it or not?

"I will whoop your ass if you do it for any reason other than because *you* want to, not to make some selfish asswipe happy." Cindy emphasized her comment by slapping Molly's shoulder. "And I ain't joking."

"Okay, okay. He knows I don't want to."

They ordered their food and paid. Grabbing her tray Molly said, "Let's change the subject. You're supposed to be making me feel better."

"Sorry. I have a new topic." Cindy led her to a corner booth. She slid across the red pleather seat, dropping her voice to a whisper. "What's going on with you and Hayden?"

Molly cleared her throat. "Nothing." She took a bite of her taco.

Cindy giggled. "Look at those red cheeks. Yeah, something's going on."

"Nothing is going on. Hayden is my friend." She shoved her taco back into her mouth.

"I hate to tell you this but there's been talk." Cindy popped a nacho into her mouth.

Molly took a drink and glared at her friend. "What talk?"

"Everybody knows Hayden likes you."

"He does not like me. He's Trevor's best friend." She frowned remembering their exchange after the race.

"Girl your blind." Cindy laughed. "Hayden looks at you like he has the lyrics to Jessie's Girl runnin' through his head." She ate another nacho.

Molly shook her head. "No way." She tried to swallow her taco, but her throat was too dry. She pushed away her food and took a drink instead.

Cindy sang, snapping her fingers and dancing in her seat. "I wanna tell her that I love her, but the point is prob'ly moot."

"Stop it. You're acting ridiculous."

Cindy laughed and leaned in again. "The point ain't moot though, is it?"

"What?" Molly took another bite of her taco. The cheese tasted like glue in her mouth.

"I mean, you like him. Hell, everybody likes him. With that hot bod and awesome hair. Mmm, mmm." Cindy fanned herself. "That's why Andrea hates you. She wants him but knows he likes you, too. *And* you kick her ass in every race."

Molly threw the last few bites of her taco on the tray. "I don't like him. Besides, I wouldn't want to be on his list of conquests."

She tried not to picture Hayden's face when he'd hugged her today. But it was there anyway. His straight white teeth smiling, his green eyes sparkling like emeralds in the sun. His hard, muscled chest pressed against hers. Though it shouldn't, her heart thumped harder when she thought of him.

No wonder Trevor had seemed mad at Hayden. No wonder he didn't trust her. She could see how Trevor might think she was flirting with Hayden. But she wasn't, was she? Another question she couldn't answer.

Cindy smiled. "He's only doing that to replace you girl. Why do you think he doesn't stay with anyone? Yep, you're a real live

Jessie's Girl." She squeezed Molly's hand. "And I'm rooting for the friend because he's the one for you."

Molly ignored Cindy's last comment. "I have to go. Come on, take me home so I can shower. I need to call Trevor. My boyfriend." Had he heard the talk, too?

Cindy pouted, pushing out her bottom lip. "I thought you wanted to hang at the arcade?"

"No. If what you say is true, I need to straighten this out with Trevor. That's probably why he's pissed at me."

"Listen." Cindy's brows furrowed into a black v over her dark brown eyes. "I want you to be happy. And I don't think Trevor is the one who does that for you. There's too much drama with him. And I'm not talking about the plays he stars in at school. Maybe Hayden could make you happy, if you give him the chance."

There were times she agreed with Cindy. Trevor was moody, and she didn't know how to talk to him. But the thought of breaking up with him hurt. When they were alone, he always knew the right things to say.

Of course, he found plenty of ways to make her feel bad, too. Like yesterday at the mall and today when he'd made her feel guilty for wanting to talk to the scouts instead of him. Was she happy with Trevor or just afraid to try something new? She had too many questions and needed answers.

"I need to talk to Trevor. I'm sure we can work this out. I have to try."

"Okay, but just keep Hayden in mind when you talk to Trevor." Cindy sighed and rolled her eyes, hands on her hips. "I know he'd treat you better, Molly. And he is too fine. You know you can't argue with that."

Molly grinned. "Is he paying you for this shameless promotion?"

Cindy snorted. "No, but if it works out in his favor, he will. Come on, I'll take you home."

CHAPTER FIVE

MOLLY

Molly closed the door of Cindy's car and turned toward the house.

Cindy stuck her head out the window and yelled, "See you later. Tell Hayden I said hi!"

Molly shook her head while Cindy drove away. She ran through the front door and past the patched, blue checkered sofa. Grabbing the chipped plaster corner of the wall, she flung herself down the hall, and dashed toward the shower.

She reached the bathroom and tore off her track sweats and uniform then cranked the rusty faucet to start the water in the shower. The old pipes groaned, water trickling out.

"Damn it." She turned it off then tried again. On the fourth attempt, the water flowed with more force. She threw her clothes into the broken wicker hamper, closed her eyes, and rubbed her temples, waiting for the shower to heat.

"What a day." It was only half over, and she already felt wiped out.

She bounced with excitement thinking about the meet. Running always left her exhilarated. It was the only place where she felt she truly belonged, the only time she knew what she had to do to get what she wanted. Her legs and feet propelled her forward toward the finish, pushed her up hills and past competitors. She had power and strength. Off the course though...

She looked around her shabby old bathroom. A tattered, green pillowcase hung on a crooked tension rod her mom got out of the neighbor's trash. It covered the cracked and dirty window. The dark brown veneer of the cabinet had gouges from the previous owners who either had a pet wolverine or an ill-mannered child with long nails and a bad temper.

The countertops and floor were matching shades of mustard yellow sprinkled with black flecks that weren't original to the plan. Molly tried not to consider what they were and pretended they belonged there.

Her mom tried to provide for them, but being a single mom was hard. Her factory job gave them enough to pay the bills, but her mom had to waitress to have money for food and necessities. The idea of Molly getting a job to help her mom out wasn't allowed.

"You need to focus on school and running. That's your golden ticket, Molly. You can get yourself out of this ditch and make something of yourself."

But the towels had holes, the walls peeled both paint and wallpaper, and the refrigerator was never full. Every time her mom came home from one job and left for the next, Molly watched her leave with a horrible ball of guilt in her empty stomach. So, she did what her mom wanted. She studied hard and ran harder. Now the effort and sacrifice were about to pay off.

Steam drifted from the shower and Molly hurried into the stall. The warm spray wouldn't last long. She rushed through her routine—wash, shampoo, condition, shave—faster than her race time. Hot water was another thing they were short on. Maybe she should invest in Nair. At least then she could take 'shave' off her list of required shower activities and have time to enjoy the hot water.

The stream cooled, and she turned the rusty handles to cut off the flow. After drying and wrapping the towel around her wet hair, she ran to her bedroom across the hall.

Pulling on a pair of black stirrup pants and a blue tunic with long, flowing sleeves, she touched the colored streak of blue in her hair. She didn't like it very much, but Trevor did. When she had asked Cindy to help her dye a blue streak in the hair on the left side of her head, Cindy had thrown a fit. Molly smiled remembering the ordeal.

"What the hell, girl. Why you wanna do that?" Cindy had snatched the box of dye from Molly's hand.

Molly shrugged. "It's cool, you know, like Cindy Lauper. Besides, Trevor likes blue."

Cindy rolled her eyes. "Girl being friends with you is like being friends with the characters on The Breakfast Club." She read the directions on the box.

Molly giggled. "Which one am I?"

Cindy had replied with a glare. "All of them. It's like you don't even know who you are. How am I supposed to figure it out?"

Molly hung out with Trevor's theater friends. Most of the girls had color in their hair. Trevor had liked it, so she had kept the streak. With Trevor's group, it was cool, with her running teams, it was weird. It was another example of how she didn't belong.

Molly hung her head upside down, scrunching her hair under the hot air from the dryer. She finished and stood, flipping her hair on the way. The curls bounced off her shoulders, one blue stripe standing out among the blond. She noticed the blue color stopped a half inch from her scalp and made a mental note to touch it up ASAP.

She sprayed Aqua Net and scrunched more. Satisfied her hair was fluffy enough, she applied mascara and lip gloss. With her long thick locks, keeping up with the big hair was easy.

The heavy eye liner and make-up everyone wore, she couldn't afford. With Cindy as a best friend though it didn't matter. Last week, she'd snuck an extra tube of mascara in the cart when her mom wasn't looking and shared it with Molly.

Done with her prep work, she went out to the kitchen and dialed Trevor's number. She hoped he would come get her, so they could talk in person. She wanted to make things right again, and the phone was too impersonal.

"Hello?" He picked up after the second ring.

"Hey, Trev. It's me."

Molly waited, chewing her lip and twirling the phone cord with her index finger.

Then his voice came through the phone. "Hi, Molly."

"So, you want to hang out tonight?" Her heartbeat filled the silence.

"I don't know. You sure you have time for me?"

She frowned. "Of course, I do. Come get me and let's go do something."

Trevor chuckled. "Well, what I want to do you won't. But I'll be there in a few."

She gulped in a deep breath. "Okay, I'm ready." He hung up without answering. Replacing the phone on the wall cradle, Molly went to wait on the porch.

After fifteen minutes, Trevor pulled into her driveway, his dark blue Camaro reflecting the late afternoon sun.

Molly swallowed to clear the fear from her throat and walked toward his car.

He sat in the car watching her approach. He'd pulled his dark blond hair back in a ponytail on the nape of his neck, her favorite style. His Oakley's flashed her way and he smiled. Her heart

fluttered in her chest. Was that love? She sat next to him in the car.

"Hi." Her stomach clenched like it did on their first date,

when she couldn't believe he wanted to be with her.

Trevor pulled the sunglasses to the bridge of his nose and

met her eyes. The smile turned to a smirk. "Yeah. We need to talk."

Her stomach fell to her feet, like being on a roller coaster

while it screamed down a hill. "Trevor, I heard what people are

saying."

"So have I." He pushed the glasses back up, blocking his

eyes.

Molly tried to take a deep breath. "You know it isn't true,

right?" This could not be happening. Not today. Everything had

finally been going right.

Trevor turned away, looking at Molly's neighborhood. She

glanced around, too, seeing the rundown houses and ill-kept yards

for the first time.

He blew out a deep breath. "I don't think we should go out

anymore. And it's not because of what people are saying." He took

off the glasses and glared into her eyes. "I don't think you care enough about me. You put other things before me and I'm sick of it, sick of being treated like I don't matter."

"That's not true. Of course you matter." She tried to breathe, but her lungs were filled with concrete. "Please, don't say that."

Trevor shook his head. His gaze dropped to his hands. "The only thing important to you is running. And I don't want to sit by and watch anymore. I have needs too but you don't care about them." He reached over to open her door. "I'm sorry. But I'm done. I need someone who cares for more than themselves."

Her eyes filled with tears. "Are you sure this has nothing to do with Hayden?"

Trevor's eyes narrowed, and his top lip twitched. "I told you it has nothing to do with him. Why do you keep bringing him up?"

Molly focused on her twisting hands. "It's just, Cindy told me everyone's saying Hayden, well, likes me and I don't want you to think it's true."

"Yeah, I heard. I'm sure my best friend wouldn't have anything to do with you either. He's smart enough to know a lost cause when he sees it."

She gasped. "What the hell. Why are you being so mean?"

"Whatever just get out. I need to go. Good luck with running, Molly. I'm sure it will take you places." He looked around again, grimacing. "I hope it takes you someplace better than here."

Molly stumbled out of the car, avoiding Trevor's eyes. Not that she could see him around the tears. She slammed the door. He hit the gas and raced away, squealing his tires on the bumpy pavement of her torn up road. She ran back inside, wiping the tears from her cheeks.

She ran to the kitchen and picked up the phone. On the third ring, Cindy answered. "Hello?"

Unable to form words, she sobbed into the phone.

Cindy said, "I'm on my way, honey."

Molly hung up, slid to the floor and waited for her friend to come and make things better.

CHAPTER SIX

HAYDEN

Hayden parked his car by the curb and put the key in his pocket. He jogged up the sidewalk to the front door of the house. Mike's sprawling brick ranch was a second home for Hayden. Since Hayden didn't burn a thousand degrees in jealousy because of Mike, he'd been here more than Trevor's house lately.

Mike's parents were out of town for the weekend and he "volunteered" to have a party. It was a loose interpretation of the word. Mike said, "Don't break anything or get me busted with the cops," and the party began.

Hayden didn't bother to knock. Nobody would hear it anyway. Loud voices and laughter came through the closed door. Inside, the living room teamed with kids from school.

He scanned the room, checking out the crowd. He needed a distraction tonight, something to get his mind off Molly. Unfortunately, the same old people were here, and the same old girls. The one he wanted to see least was the first to greet him.

"Hi, Hayden." Andrea slid up to his side and grabbed his arm. "I didn't know you were *coming* tonight." She turned him toward her and moved her hands to his waist.

He raised an eyebrow at the suggestion in her words, pulling away from her grasp. "Andrea, no amount of beer will make that happen. Your brother was mad enough with our one date."

"Who cares what Tim thinks." She moved closer, rubbing Hayden's chest. "Come on, Hayden. He doesn't have to know."

"Tim isn't the reason I'm not interested." Hayden lowered his voice. "Why don't you go find Trevor? He's already been interested from what I hear."

Andrea narrowed her eyes, pushing Hayden away. "Fuck you."

He laughed. "No, thanks."

Andrea scowled and stormed away.

Hayden sighed. Maybe he'd have a beer instead. He could kill a few brain cells and numb his pain. He could always sleep it off in the spare bedroom and go home tomorrow.

"Hayden!" Mike called over the music from across the room. He stood by the keg, squirting beer into the red cups everyone was holding. Mike smiled and raised a red cup to Hayden.

Hayden smiled too and walked over. "Hey, Mike. I see your brother, Tony, is watching you while your parents are in Mexico." Hayden pointed to the keg.

Mike laughed. "My big brother takes good care of me."

"Yes, he's doing a great job." Hayden raised his cup in a salute.

Mike grinned. "I saw Andrea, uh, talking to you."

"That girl's a mess. I hope you took her keys."

Mike shrugged, pouring another cup. "She came with Tim. She's his problem, not mine."

A flash of blue caught Hayden's eye and Molly stumbled in from the kitchen. He stared, open-mouthed, while she tripped through the living room. She walked behind the sectional couch toward the keg, holding on to the leather back for support. He set his beer on an end table and rushed over to help her.

"Molly, what the hell are you doing?" He grabbed her by the shoulders and turned her face to him.

Her gray eyes filled with tears. For one moment, the tears sparkled like diamonds, then they spilled over onto her cheeks. She threw herself at Hayden. He caught her, and she sobbed on his chest. He tried not to think about how good her body felt.

Mike frowned and shook his head at Hayden. "Don't do it, man."

"I'm not doing anything." Hayden couldn't believe Molly would drink, let alone get so wasted. "Where's Trevor?"

Mike shrugged. "He's not here."

Andrea stood behind Mike, smirking. She met Hayden's glare and raised her cup. Her narrowed gaze landed on Molly's shaking shoulders. "Someone can't handle their alcohol."

Hayden glared at Andrea. "Shut up. Maybe it's because she's not a lush. Could that be why she always beats you?"

He winced at the hurt on Andrea's face but Molly was his priority.

Molly still gripped the front of Hayden's shirt. Mike looked at her then shook his head.

"Come on, Molly." Hayden pulled her through the kitchen and into the guest room he'd slept in before. He shut the door and sat with her on the edge of the bed.

"Molly, what's wrong? Where's Trevor?" He lifted her chin with his finger.

More tears fell, and Molly sniffled. "I don't know. I came with Cindy. Trevor dumped me today." She closed her eyes and dropped her chin to her chest.

Hayden closed his eyes and shook his head. Trevor was an idiot. How could he hurt her like this? Wait… he was the idiot. Who cared why Trevor broke up with her, she was free.

"I'm sorry he hurt you." He hugged her to his chest. The earlier guilt melted away with the heat of her touch. He leaned his head on her silky hair. The smell of strawberries filled his nose.

"He didn't even give me a chance to defend myself. He said I didn't care enough about his needs and left." She sniffled. "I thought it was because of you, but he said it wasn't."

Whoa, wait a minute. Does she mean… Hayden's hopes skyrocketed. He held her by the shoulders. "What do you mean because of me?"

Molly's cheeks turned pink. "Because everyone is saying you like me. That's stupid. You're my friend."

Hayden gritted his teeth. Mike wasn't the only one who noticed. But if it was so obvious, why didn't Molly see it? His hopes nosedived back to earth. She didn't notice because she didn't feel the same way. "Let me take you home. Where is Cindy?"

She blinked a few times. "I don't know. Out there I guess." She pointed to the door. "I'm so tired, Hayden." She closed her eyes and leaned onto his chest.

Hayden held her for a minute, her body soft and warm against his. He ached for something more than friendship. "Come on. Let's find Cindy and I'll get you out of here."

The heat from her sigh brushed his neck. He wished it were her lips instead. *Tonight totally sucks.*

"Okay, Hayden." Molly tightened her arms around his back and grew still.

"Molly?" Hayden waited for a response. Her soft sleepy breaths echoed against his chest and he sighed.

If anyone saw this, the jokes about Hayden, the player, boring the girl of his dreams to sleep would be the joke of the school. But he couldn't let her go. He'd wanted to hold her in his arms for so long, and it didn't matter to him she was passed out drunk. This might be the only chance he got.

But it would matter to her if everyone knew. He gently pushed her away, holding her face between his hands. A small quiet sigh escaped her lips, and Hayden caressed her soft cheeks. She was so beautiful it made his stomach hurt. Damn it, why couldn't she like him?

"Molly wake up. I'll take you home, but you have to walk to my car."

Her eyes fluttered open and her long lashes sparkled with her tears. Before Hayden could move, she leaned in and kissed him.

He moaned and kissed her back. She tasted incredible. Her cherry flavored lips made his heart pound like an Alex Van Halen drum solo.

She rubbed her fingers in his hair, breathing fast. Hayden let go of her cheeks and slid his hands to her back. She arched toward him, pressing herself closer. He imagined pushing her onto the bed and living out one of his daydreams. But this was just a drunk kiss. She didn't mean it. He pulled away before she could reject him.

She opened her eyes. "Hayden, I…" More tears flooded her cheeks.

Hayden leaned his forehead on hers. "I'm sorry, Molly. I shouldn't have done that." He pulled her off the bed. "Let's go. I'll drive you home."

Molly nodded. She stumbled toward the door, and Hayden steadied her with a hand on her shoulder, fighting the urge to lead her back to the bed. Not that he'd done it before. And he knew she wasn't like that because Trevor complained enough. But it didn't stop how he felt.

He opened the door, thankful nobody was there to see them come out of a bedroom together. He hadn't thought of that when he led her there. They'd needed the quiet.

Before they got through the kitchen, Cindy ran in. "Omigod, Molly. I got stuck playing Nintendo with Mike's little brother and lost track of time. He's good. I couldn't let the little twerp beat me."

Molly stumbled again, and Cindy gasped. She sniffed in front of Molly's face. "Have you been drinking?" Cindy's narrowed glare fell on Hayden.

He held up his hands. "I found her like this. I was about to take her home." Molly teetered, and Hayden caught her, placing an arm around her waist. She smiled and leaned her head on his shoulder.

Cindy smirked. "I got her. You can help me get her outside then I'll take her home."

"If you want to stay at the party, I can take her. I haven't been drinking, honest."

Cindy snorted. "Right, and I'm sure you won't take advantage of her." She reached for Molly's arm, trying to pull her away from Hayden.

"Cindy, it's okay. Hayden won't hurt me. He's my friend."

Hayden grimaced at the words "my friend."

Cindy glared. "Boy, you better not mess with her. If I find out you do, you'll be in for a whole world of hurt." She glanced around the empty room. "I took your side earlier today, don't make me regret it."

Hayden raised his eyebrows and chuckled. "Thanks." His smile faded. "But I think my feelings are one-sided."

Cindy crossed her arms over her chest and lifted her chin. "You might be surprised. But you won't be finding out tonight. Wait til she's sober."

"What are you guys talking about. Who's on the side of sober?"

Cindy rolled her eyes. "Not you. I'm coming over tomorrow to make you run this shit out of your system. You're gonna be sorry you did this. And you ain't never doing it again."

Molly nodded and smiled at Cindy. "Okay, see you tomorrow. I love you."

Hayden laughed but Cindy shook her head. "Get her home and don't let her mother see her. She shouldn't be home until midnight, so you have an hour."

"Don't worry. I'll take care of her. That's what friends are for, right?" Hayden tried to smile but only half his mouth followed directions.

Cindy's glare softened. "Yes, and she needs a friend right now. That's what matters."

Hayden smiled a real smile this time. "Yeah, you're right. See you later." He led Molly out the back door and around the side of the house to his car.

The drive to her house was absolute torture. She slept in the passenger seat. He tried to stay calm when she leaned over and laid her head on his shoulder. When she rested her hand on his leg, he swallowed hard then placed it on her lap. She sighed in her sleep and mumbled something Hayden couldn't make out. But his heart sped faster as his name fell from her lips.

Hayden pulled into her driveway. He walked around the car and pulled open the passenger door. "Molly, we're at your house. Come on, wake up." He rubbed her arm.

She sighed but didn't wake up. Reaching in, Hayden unbuckled her seatbelt. He slid one arm under her knees and the other behind her back and carried her inside. He placed her on her bed.

Cindy's threat echoed through his thoughts and he chuckled softly. It would be too easy to take advantage of Molly now, but Hayden would never do that to anyone, especially not the girl he loved.

Unable to leave without something, Hayden leaned over and kissed Molly's forehead. "Good night, Molly."

He smiled when she snuggled into her pillow. She never woke up, but when he turned to leave, she whispered his name. He fought the desire to stay. Instead he smiled again and closed the door.

CHAPTER SEVEN

MOLLY

Monday at school, Molly walked through the hall dodging the stares of her classmates. Cindy did the opposite and glared back.

Hugging her books to her chest she whispered, "Cindy, are you sure nothing happened at the party? Why is everyone looking at me?"

Cindy sighed. "I told you, Hayden drove you home. I don't know what the hell they're trippin' about."

They reached their English class and took their seats in the back of the room. Molly glanced around. Several kids were there, talking to friends while they waited for class to begin.

Andrea glared at her. Molly looked away and leaned closer to Cindy. "I think Hayden and I kissed. I don't remember much, but I remember that. Do you think he told someone?"

"That lying bastard. I told him not to take advantage of you. I'll whoop his ass." Cindy looked toward the door.

"No, that's not what I meant." Molly whispered even softer. "*I* kissed *him*."

"What?" Cindy grabbed Molly's hands, eyes wide. "Why you didn't tell me this yesterday? It's about time girl. What did he do? What did he say? How was it? I'll bet he's better than you know who."

Molly frowned avoiding Cindy's eyes. "That's just it. I remember kissing him, but I passed out right after." She laid her head on the desk and groaned. "Is it possible to have a hang over two days after drinking?"

Cindy giggled. "It serves you right. That was the dumbest thing you've done."

Molly shrugged. "I was upset because of Trevor. Everyone kept asking about him and Mike handed me a cup. You weren't there to tell me not to do it I guess, so I drank."

Cindy shook a finger in Molly's face. "You're smarter than that. That's not you, Molly, giving in to peer pressure."

"I don't know, maybe it is me. I let you tell me what to do." She sighed. "You were right. I don't know who I am." A tear trickled down Molly's cheek. She wiped it away with her sleeve.

Cindy squeezed her hand. "Molly, you're a strong, fierce competitor. That's who you are, on or off the course. Have some confidence."

Molly nodded. Hayden walked into the room. He met her gaze and smiled. Molly's heart flip-flopped in her chest as he took his seat in front of her.

"Hey, Molly. What's up, Cindy?" Hayden greeted them like nothing out of the ordinary had happened. Like he hadn't freaking carried Molly's drunk ass into her bedroom and tucked her in two nights before. Like she hadn't thrown herself at him and kissed him the same day his best friend dumped her.

Molly pulled out her notebook and doodled on the cover. "Hi."

If he liked her, he would be embarrassed, wouldn't he? His eyes wouldn't meet hers with cocky confidence. His chest would be tight like hers and he'd be afraid to look at her like she was afraid to look at him. Her face heated from her stupidity. He was just a friend, nothing more.

Cindy's gaze bounced between them. She turned to Hayden. "So, thanks for taking my drunk friend home Saturday night. I hope she wasn't too much trouble."

Molly jerked her hand and tore a hole in the paper. She glared at her so-called best friend.

"It was no problem, she slept on the way home." He turned in his seat to look at Molly. "Did you know you talk in your sleep?"

Molly groaned. "Yes. What did I say?"

Hayden shrugged, chuckling. "Well, maybe you sleep mumble. The only word I understood was my name."

Oh my God. Why couldn't the desk swallow her whole, like the bed in *A Nightmare on Elm Street* swallowed the mom?

Cindy barked out a loud laugh. "I hear her talk about running when we sleep over at each other's houses. Sometimes food. It's always the things she wants most."

Hayden laughed, too.

Molly lifted her head, trying not to kick Cindy. "Tonight, I'll be talking about a scholarship. That's what I want most." She narrowed her eyes at Cindy and mouthed *stop*.

Cindy shook her head. "That's not what you need most though."

"It's the only way I can go to college, so it tops my need list." Molly looked at Hayden. Time for a new topic. "Are you playing soccer at college?"

His emerald eyes twinkled. "No, it's fun but I'm not that serious about it. Not like you are with running. Where do you want to run?"

She slouched a little in her chair. "The scouts from UCLA and U of I are interested. I guess whichever one makes the best offer." She frowned. "That is if they make one."

"You'll get offers from both." He patted her hand, his lingered on hers for a moment. Then he pulled it away, dragging his fingers along the back of her hand.

"Thanks. I hope so." Molly checked her hand for smoke. "If I do, I wouldn't mind going to California. I've always wanted to go there."

Hayden agreed. "I've been there, it's nice. UCLA would be great."

"Have you applied anywhere?" Cindy asked.

"To a few places, but I haven't picked one yet." Hayden tilted his head. "How about you?"

She smirked. "I'm going to major in Psychology. I'm good at helping others with their problems. I'll probably follow Molly. She may need help making good choices. Saturday was an example of what she does on her own."

Hayden raised an eyebrow but didn't comment.

Molly glared at her. "Whatever. I think I can handle it. Saturday was just a bad day, that's all."

Cindy shrugged. "If you say so. I'll be right back. I need to talk to Mrs. Richter about our research paper." She walked to the front of the class to the teacher's desk.

Trevor walked through the door and took his seat at the front of the classroom. Molly frowned, her stomach clenching. He didn't even look at her, instead he smiled and laughed with Andrea who sat next to him. Pain filled her stomach like a red-hot bubble. The awful things he said came back to her.

Andrea glanced at her and leaned in toward Trevor to whisper something. His back stiffened, and he turned to glare at Molly.

Molly looked away, heat creeping into her face. "Oh no." The whisper shook on the way out of her throat. "Was Andrea at the party Saturday?"

Hayden grimaced. "Yes, she teased you about drinking and not handling your alcohol. Don't you remember?"

Molly shook her head. "There aren't many things I remember about Saturday night. Did she see us together?" The stares, the whispering, it made sense now.

"Well, yeah. I told her off for making fun of you." He blushed. "Sorry, but she was being a total bitch."

She glanced at Andrea whispering in Trevor's ear again. "Did she see us leave together?"

"Nobody did. I took you out the back door." He swallowed, his gaze falling to the desk between them. "Molly, do you remember… talking in the bedroom at Mike's?"

Butterflies bombarded her stomach. She was drunk that night for the first, and hopefully last, time. Things were blurry. But she had lied to Cindy. She remembered everything about the kiss.

The softness of Hayden's lips, him holding her face, the warmth that flooded her body, the spark, the magic. She tingled now thinking about it. Imagining his lips moving with hers, she took a breath and whispered, "I remember."

Hayden stared intently into her eyes. "And what does that mean? Do you remember everything? And does it matter to you?"

She tried to swallow, to breathe, to blink. She should tell him no. She didn't want him to know her feelings when he didn't share them.

Lie. Lie and tell him it was just a drunk kiss.

But even as she gave herself the command, she blurted out her answer. "I remember everything. And yes, it matters. At least, it does to me."

She bounced her legs under the desk. Where was Cindy? She usually stopped her from saying stupid things. Cheeks on fire, she twisted her hands on the desktop.

Now Hayden would have a good laugh and she would look like a total idiot.

But Hayden didn't laugh. He leaned his forehead on hers and covered her hands with his, caressing her skin.

Molly gasped softly and focused on their hands.

Hayden whispered, "Good, because it's mattered to me ever since we met. Trevor's not right for you. I can treat you better. Will you let me try?"

Oh. My. God.

Molly closed her eyes, struggling to draw a breath. Hayden *did* like her. She opened her mouth to answer and the pressure of Hayden's head disappeared.

"What the hell are you doing, Hayden?" Trevor shoved Hayden away from Molly. "I thought you were my best friend. Get the hell away from her."

Hayden fell backward, grabbing the desk. Then, he jumped, pushing Trevor into Cindy's empty desk. Trevor and the desk crashed to the floor.

Hayden shouted back. "Don't touch me. And you broke up with her, so it's not up to you."

"Boys, stop. Right now!" Mrs. Richter rushed over to get between Hayden and Trevor. With the shoulder pads on her beige blazer, she looked like a football linebacker in a skirt. Hayden towered over Trevor while he untangled himself from the overturned desk on the floor.

Molly stood with their teacher. She put her hand on Hayden's chest. "Please, stop."

Everyone in class sat open-mouthed, watching the fight. Andrea laughed, other kids stared and snickered. Why couldn't movies be real? Then maybe the floor would open and take her.

"Boys, to the office. Now. Everyone work on your research until I get back. Molly, you come with us." Mrs. Richter walked to the door. "Let's go." She marched into the hall, her heels clicking on the tile.

Trevor pulled himself up glaring at Hayden. He yanked his backpack from the chair and followed their teacher.

Cindy winked and gave her a thumb's up. Molly shook her head.

Hayden touched her arm. "Come on." He slung his bag over his shoulder and headed to the door, grinning. "I think I may be out of school the next couple days. Will you bring my homework?"

She walked with him and rolled her eyes. "You're an idiot, Hayden." Then she grinned back. "But sure, I'll get it for you."

"Thanks." He smiled, and they followed Trevor and Mrs. Richter. He touched her back to guide her through the door and she shivered. In the hall, Hayden pulled her to a stop with a hand on her shoulder.

"By the way." He caressed her cheek, an emerald fire twinkling in his eye. "I'm not finished fighting for you."

He kissed her softly, sending her heart into her throat.

"Mr. Bishop," their teacher called, "unless you want to add to your suspension for inappropriate behavior, let's go."

Hayden chuckled. Only when he grabbed her hand to lead her toward the office did Molly breathe again.

Did she want Hayden to fight for her? She pictured the hurt on Trevor's face when he and Hayden yelled at each other. Her fault. The guilt was hard to ignore.

Was he upset because he wanted to get back together or was he mad because his friend hurt him? Did she still like Trevor? When she remembered what Trevor had said, she wasn't sure she'd take him back.

Only one thing was certain, Trevor had never made her breathless the way Hayden did. But were her feelings for Hayden real or were they just another manifestation of her uncertainty? She didn't know. And the best Molly could offer Hayden, or herself, was maybe.

Would that be enough?

CHAPTER EIGHT

HAYDEN

Foot tapping, eyes glaring, Trevor epitomized the phrase "if looks could kill."

"What the hell. Why were you hitting on my girlfriend?"

Hayden raised his eyebrows. "Girlfriend? You broke up with her. She's fair game now."

Screw the bro code. Trevor was less and less like a "bro" every day. The way he treated Molly disgusted Hayden. And she didn't even know half of what Trevor had said and done.

"It wasn't official yet. Maybe I changed my mind. You should have waited before you moved in on her." Trevor crossed his arms and leaned back in the chair. "I was about to tell her I was sorry. And that I'd take her back."

Hayden balled his hands into fists. "What makes you think she wants to have you back? You've always treated her like shit."

Trevor chuckled. "Oh, she'd come back."

Hayden spoke softly through clenched teeth. "Not if she knew about the cheating."

Trevor leaned forward on the chair. "You better not fucking tell her, Hayden. That's not cool."

Hayden's laugh was sarcastic. "Right, not cool. Cheating on your girlfriend is though. You don't deserve her. And *Molly* deserves better."

The door to the principal's office opened and Molly walked out. They both stood, and Hayden took a step closer to her. She met his eyes then Trevor's.

"Hayden, you need to go in now." She continued to stare at Trevor with a frown.

"Molly, you didn't get in trouble, did you?" She stared at Trevor and Hayden's gut turned.

She gazed at Trevor for another moment then answered Hayden. Her gray gaze moved over his face, avoiding his eyes. "No. He wanted my side of the story. I have to go back to class." Hayden waited for her to leave. He didn't want Trevor to have time alone with her.

Molly gestured to the door. "You'd better go. He's already mad." She finally met his eyes.

Hayden didn't move. He wanted to touch her and see the warm gaze from when he kissed her.

"Go." She grinned. "I'll bring your homework later."

Instead of relief, fear raked its icy claws on Hayden's back, like a wet Gremlin in the kitchen after midnight.

Molly's gaze bounced back to Trevor.

"Let's go Mr. Bishop. I haven't got all day." Mr. Roberts' voice boomed from his office.

Hayden smiled at Molly to hide his fear. "I'll see you later. Call me and I can come pick it up."

She nodded, and Hayden entered the office. He glanced at Trevor's face before the door closed. The look Trevor gave Molly could win an Oscar. Even *he* almost believed Trevor was sorry. *Guess those acting lessons paid off.* Hayden grimaced. This fight wasn't over yet, and he would find a way to win.

***

Hayden waited by the phone later that night. Molly's practice had ended an hour ago, and he expected to hear the ring of his phone. She hadn't called.

She's got five more minutes until I go to her house.

Hayden had told himself this for the last half hour. But he stayed put, afraid if he left, he might miss her call and maybe she'd call Trevor instead.

When the five minutes were up, Hayden groaned and threw himself back on the bed.

His head bounced on the pillows. "Fuck."

Hayden covered his eyes. He raised up to get off the bed and the ring of his phone shook his ear drums. He grabbed it, knocking the cradle off the nightstand by his bed.

He took a breath and answered. "Hello?"

"Hi, Hayden."

He smiled, the pain and fear melting when she said his name. "Hi, Molly. How's it going?" He tried not to sound like he'd been waiting for her to call.

"I have your homework. Can I bring it over? My mom is at work and she doesn't allow boys over here when I'm alone."

"How will you get here?" His parents weren't home either, but they didn't have the same rule.

"Cindy. She and I are going to her house to study." She sighed. "I'm sorry you got suspended."

Hayden snorted into the phone. "Yeah, my parents are pissed. Mostly my mom though. My dad understood. Once I told him the reason."

Silence came from Molly's end. He only heard her soft breathing. "Molly?"

"We can talk when I get there. I'll be there in a few minutes."

The Gremlin tapped on Hayden's back again. "Sure, see you soon."

Hayden waited for her in the living room. The lights from Cindy's car flashed through his mom's lacy white curtains. Holding his breath, he bounced on his toes waiting for the ring of the doorbell.

The sound of her footsteps climbing their porch steps vibrated in his bones. She rang, and he pulled the door open, smiling. She returned the smile. A good sign.

"Hey." She sounded breathless, like she'd been running.

"Hey, come on in." He stepped back to make room.

She glanced back at the car. "I can't. Cindy's waiting." She held out his books and a folder.

Hayden glanced into the driver's seat. Cindy smiled at him and waved, gesturing for him to go inside. Hayden nodded.

"Just come in for a minute so we can talk." He took his things from her and touched her arm.

Molly opened then closed her mouth but stepped into the house.

Hayden closed the door and placed the books on the entry table. "Come sit on the couch." He grinned at her worried face. "I won't bite."

She laughed a shaky laugh. "That's what they all say." She joined him on the couch. Her strawberry scented hair played with the rhythm of his heart.

He grabbed her hands, rubbing her smooth skin with his thumbs.

She wiggled on the couch, adjusting her shoulders. "I don't think we should…"

"Stop. Please, give me a chance." He reached up and rubbed one hand down her hair, tracing the blue streak. "What are you afraid of?"

She looked at the hand he still held. "I'm confused. I don't know what I want. It's not fair to you." She lifted her eyes to his.

"I've known Trevor my whole life, and you deserve better." He caressed her face. "Please, just try."

Tears filled her eyes. Hayden wanted to tell her everything Trevor had done. The lying, the cheating, the things Trevor said about her with the guys when he thought Hayden wasn't around. But he didn't want to hurt her more.

"Hayden, you're my friend. What if I hurt you? I don't want to lose our friendship."

"You can't put me in the friend zone. It's too late." He leaned his face toward her. She didn't back away, so he continued until he tasted her lips. She moaned and wrapped her arms around his neck.

Hayden slipped his hands around her back. The heat from their kiss melted away all his earlier fear and doubt. How many times had he daydreamed about kissing her like this? Too many. To have it happen was better than a dream come true. It was like winning the lottery and getting everything you ever wished for.

Molly slid her hands to his chest. Her touch left him breathless, he wanted her to touch him more. But then, she pushed him away and he frowned.

He swallowed, trying to slow his breathing and stared into the silvery glow of her eyes. "Molly I love you."

"Don't say that." She blinked, and the tears fell.

Tears weren't the reaction he wanted to see. He reached up to wipe them away. "It's how I feel. I wanted to tell you, so you could see I'm serious about you. I've loved you for a long time."

She jumped off the couch. Hayden followed, holding her shoulders to keep her from running. He smiled. "Don't run from me. I can't catch you."

"I have to go. Cindy's waiting."

She tried to pull away, but Hayden held her tight. "Do you like me?"

She closed her eyes, and bit lower lip. "Yes, Hayden, but I'm confused."

He kissed her again, letting his hands slide down her arms to her hands. "I'm not. I want you. I've always wanted you."

She gazed at him, her eyebrows folding together. "Why?"

Hayden smiled at her question. "Because, you're funny, you're smart, you like the things I like, and laugh at my stupid jokes." He brought her fingers to his mouth and kissed her knuckles. "And you're beautiful. Inside and out."

"You must see someone else." She stepped back.

Hayden shook his head. "Please, don't go." The space between them widened, his heart rate increasing with every inch. He was losing the fight.

She shook her head. "I have to."

"I'm not giving up." The words were a promise for them both.

She gave him a sad smile. "You should. You don't know me. I don't even know myself."

"Wait." He took a step, and she rushed out the door. By the time he made it to the porch, she had jumped into Cindy's car and slammed the door.

Hayden sighed. *Damn she's fast.*

Cindy met his eyes through the windshield and shook her head. At least Hayden knew he had back up. Maybe Cindy would help him convince Molly to give him a chance.

As they pulled away, Hayden sank onto the porch swing. He never would have believed three days off from school could sound like absolute torture. At least Trevor wouldn't be there either, the only bright spot in this fucking mess.

CHAPTER NINE

MOLLY

Thursday after practice, Cindy drove Molly home. In the driveway, Molly sighed and reached for the door handle, but Cindy grabbed her arm.

"Tomorrow they'll both be back at school. What are you going to do?"

Cindy had asked her this question ten times a day. Molly gave the same answer. "I don't know."

Each time she thought about Trevor and Hayden, she switched between giving Hayden a chance and getting back together with Trevor.

Cindy groaned. "You know what I think, girl. I don't know why you even think there's a choice. You know who you belong with."

She glared at Cindy. "If I knew, this wouldn't be so hard."

Cindy rolled her eyes so hard they were white. "It's a no brainer. Hayden. *Pick Hayden.* Trevor is an asshole and a liar and he's playin' with you."

"You've never liked Trevor, Cindy. But you don't know him. He's not playing with me, he's just…" She searched for the right word. "Unsure, like me. He's trying to figure out who he is."

Cindy raised her eyebrows, her jaw open. Then she laughed. "That boy knows who he is and what he's doing. I'd bet he lies awake at night thinking of ways to mess with your emotions."

Molly grunted and got out of the car. She leaned through the opening. "He's not what you think. And he's not playing with me."

Cindy laughed again. "Molly, he's Pat Sajak and you're Vanna White. Trevor's got you spinnin' on the wheel. You need to jump off and let Hayden catch you."

Slamming the door, Molly glared and ran into the house while Cindy backed out and drove away, still laughing. Sometimes Cindy was so mean. Molly loved her, but right now she didn't like her very much.

Molly threw her backpack on the counter and went to the pantry to get something started for dinner. Slamming a few cabinets didn't help forget Hayden, Trevor, and Cindy, but it made her feel better.

She grabbed the ingredients for spaghetti. Once the noodles were boiling and the sauce warming in pan, she pulled out her homework. Cindy would deliver Hayden's—under protest—but avoiding Hayden herself made more sense.

She completed her math before dinner was ready. When her mom pulled in the driveway, she dished two plates and sat them on the table as her mom opened the door.

"Hey, Mom. How was your day?" She smiled, assessing her mom's face. Even with rings around her eyes, grease covered work clothes, and blond hair escaping her loose ponytail, her mom's beauty glowed.

Molly wished for the hundredth time her dad was still around to take care of them.

"Mine was great. How was yours?" She hung her coat on the back of one of the metal folding chairs they used at the kitchen table.

Molly shrugged. "You know, same old same old." She took a bite of spaghetti. The sauce dripped on her chin.

Her mom handed her a napkin. "And practice?" She twisted her noodles on her fork and took a bite.

"It was good. I'm ready for Saturday." At least she had that going for her.

"Good. I'm trying to get off work, so I can come watch." Her mom smiled. "I'd like to see you win sectionals."

She groaned but smiled at her mom. "Don't jinx me. I only need to make the top five to go to state." She sprinkled more parmesan onto her pasta. "That's the goal."

Her mom nodded. "Well, I hope I can be there."

"If you can't be there in person, you'll be there with me inside. I take you every time." She didn't want her mom to feel guilty. But having her mom there would ease her nerves about the scouts.

They ate in silence for a few minutes then her mom sighed. "I have good news. I got a raise today."

Molly clapped and giggled. "That's great, Mom. How much? Is it enough for you to quit waitressing at the truck stop?"

Her mom shook her head. "No, it's only a ten-cent raise, but every little bit helps. I still have to waitress."

"I'm proud of you, Mom."

They finished eating and Molly stood to clean up the dishes. Her mom touched her arm. "Let's do something special to celebrate. Want to get frozen yogurt?"

The tension in Molly's chest lightened. Her mom never got to relax. But, Wednesday nights her mom always worked at the truck stop. She checked the clock.

"Don't you have to work in an hour? Will we have time?"

"Well, I don't have to go to the truck stop." Her mom's smile faded. "They let me go yesterday."

The air left Molly's chest. No waitressing meant more sacrifices. Her mom already sacrificed enough. "What happened?"

Her mom sighed. "They've been losing business since Denny's opened across the highway and since I was last hired…"

"You're the first fired." She hugged her mom. "I'm sorry. Cross-country is almost over. I can get a job and help out."

Her mom shook her head. "No. Before your father died, he made me promise to take care of you. He wanted the same thing I do, Molly, for you to be happy and successful. You need to focus on your future. You can't do that if you have to worry about work instead of homework."

Molly sighed, looking away. Her mom didn't mention her dad often. When she did, her mom's face would tighten, and her shoulders would sink lower. She didn't share the pain, her dad died when she was two and she never knew him. But she hurt for her mom and hated to argue with her.

"But, Mom…"

"Molly, no." She smiled. "Come on. I want to get frozen yogurt. TCBY is calling my name."

Molly bit her lip. Maybe her mom needed this to cheer her up. "Fine, but I get to drive."

"Deal." Her mom reached into her purse and handed Molly the keys.

Their ten-year-old Pontiac took a few tries to start, but once it did, Molly pulled out of the driveway. She loved driving, but she rarely got to do it. She parked in the lot and they went inside.

The warm smell of fresh baked waffles drifted through the store, making Molly's mouth water. She smiled at her mom. "I want two scoops of chocolate."

Her mom laughed. "Me, too. Let's hurry, this smell is driving my taste buds crazy."

They ordered and paid the perky cashier. Waffle cones in hand, they found a booth. The rich chocolate taste exploded on Molly's tongue. She bit into the side of her cone and moaned. "Thanks, Mom. This is great. Though we should be saving money now that you don't have the waitressing job."

Her mom waved a hand. "I'll get another one. Those jobs are easy to find."

"Yeah, because waitressing was hard, and nobody wants to do it. You know, I have to save money for college. If I get the scholarship, they won't give me spending money. I'd like to have fun." She winked at her mom. "College isn't supposed to be all work. I should—"

Her mom laughed. "Don't worry, I thought of that and I have a nest egg for you."

Molly gaped at her mom. "Mom, I meant I needed to get a job and save it, not you."

"Well, now you don't." She licked her cone. "I don't want to talk about money. I think you have something else we need to discuss."

Molly cleared her throat. "Oh, what's that?"

"I got a phone call from your principal."

Molly fumbled her cone but caught it before it hit the table. "You did?"

Her mom nodded. She touched Molly's hand. "Tell me what's going on."

She never hid things from her mom, but she hadn't even seen her since the fight, until tonight. Most kids hid things from their parents, but not Molly.

She told her about Trevor breaking up with her, Hayden saying he loved her, and even how she'd gotten drunk at the party and that Hayden had to bring her home.

Her mom listened, eyebrows furrowed. She nodded, frowned, and shook her head. When Molly finished, her mom sighed and patted her hand.

"I know I'm not around enough to help you, and I'm glad you can tell me these things. I'm disappointed you drank at the party.

That was dangerous. If Hayden hadn't been there, someone with less morals might have found you instead. You're lucky, he sounds like a nice boy."

Hot tears prickled Molly's eyes. "He is, Mom."

Her mom sighed. "And Trevor? Do you still like him?"

"I don't know." She laid her head on the table. "I don't know what to do."

Her mom reached over and rubbed Molly's hair, just like she used to do when Molly was little and had skinned her knee or lost a doll.

"Maybe you need to tell them both to give you space. If they both mean what they say, they'll wait, and you can decide when you're ready. If not, then neither one was meant to be." Her mom smiled. "And they wouldn't deserve you, anyway."

She considered her mom's words. Maybe it was time to focus on herself. Who was she? And what did she want? Those two questions ballooned in her mind until they pushed out everything else. Her doubt, her uncertainty, her desire to belong, none of it mattered. Her mom was right. She needed to do this alone before she could think about sharing herself.

Molly raised her head and smiled through the tears. "Thanks, Mom. That's the best advice I've had yet."

Her mom grinned. "Glad I could help. But promise me you won't drink again."

Molly laughed. "Don't worry, one hangover was enough to last a lifetime." She hugged her mom. "Besides, Cindy would whoop my ass."

Her mom laughed, too, and licked her cone. "I've always liked that girl."

CHAPTER TEN

HAYDEN

The sun reflected off the window of Cindy's car as she pulled into Hayden's driveway. Hayden ran to the door and held his breath.

He couldn't stop the brick of disappointment from dropping in his stomach when Cindy got out to carry his homework to the door. "Damn it."

He opened the door and Cindy smirked. "Sorry, it's just me."

Hayden laughed. "Thanks." He took his homework and sighed. "How was school today?"

"Same shit, different day." Cindy leaned against the door frame, crossing her arms. "She's driving me crazy too, Hayden. I don't know what the hell she's thinking."

He frowned. "What do you mean?"

Cindy looked at her feet. "She's talking to Trevor again. Well, she talked to him on the phone last night while I was at her house." She narrowed her eyes. "I know he's your BFF, but he's an ass. He's shitty to her."

Hayden stepped out and closed the door. He walked to the swing and Cindy sat with him. Rubbing his hands through his hair, he groaned. "I know, Cindy. Dammit, why is she talking to him?"

"I don't know. She said he's *different* when nobody is around." Cindy huffed and crossed her arms. "Convenient for him."

"What should I do? She doesn't belong with him." Hayden held his head in his hands. "This sucks."

Cindy patted him on the shoulder. "Trust me. I'm working on it. Just don't give up on her."

He raised his head. "I couldn't do that if I wanted to." His cheeks prickled with heat.

Cindy smiled. "You sound like a little old man, pining for his lost love. Most stud athletes don't act this way you know."

He grimaced, looking at his feet. "Yeah, don't tell. I'd never live it down." Molly would have made fun of him, too.

They sat for a minute. Cindy pushed the swing with her feet then jumped with a squeal. Hayden reached out to catch her, but she turned to face him, her eyes open wide.

"I got it," she said. "You need to go there right now and demand that she talks to you."

"Demand?" Hayden stared at her like she asked him to run naked around the block. "Don't you *know* her, Cindy? She'd slam the door in my face and never talk to me again."

Molly would never let him talk to her like that. Trevor got away with it though. He always bossed her around.

Cindy rolled her eyes and put her hands on her hips. "I mean go there and don't let her tell you no. Flash those puppy dog eyes, smile your sexy smile, bat your eyelashes, shake your ass. Do whatever it takes."

Hayden laughed despite the fear coiling like a slinky in his stomach. "Shake my ass? I don't think my break-dance moves will impress her."

"Whatever. Just go there and fight. Don't you want her?"

Hayden breathed deep. Pain flashed through him, every nerve ending igniting with fire. "I've wanted her since I first saw her."

Cindy drew herself up, shoulders squared, and chin held high. "Then go get her. Don't let Trevor steal her from you again."

"You'll make a great psychologist." Hayden smiled at Cindy. "Why are you helping me?"

Cindy's eyebrows arched over her dark brown eyes. "You? I'm doing this for her. I know you're the one for her, not Trevor." She ran down the steps and skipped away. Hayden chuckled as he watched her go.

***

Hayden drove to Molly's house like Richard Petty in the Daytona 500. He had to talk her out of getting back together with his former best friend.

He pulled up to Molly's house, the first stars just visible in the purple sunset sky. Hayden took the steps two at a time and rang the doorbell. He shifted his weight from foot to foot.

"Please, answer, Molly," he whispered, hoping she wasn't with Trevor. The door opened and her pale, sweet face greeted him. He sighed with relief.

She raised her eyebrows. "Hayden, what are you doing here? I don't have your homework, Cindy took it." Half her body peeked out through the door.

"Yeah she brought it. I didn't come here for that." He frowned at the way she hid. "I came to see you. Can I come in?"

Molly looked at the porch, nodding. "My mom went to the store. She'll be back soon but we have time to talk." She stepped back and swung the door open, avoiding his eyes.

Hayden entered like he was walking to the gallows. *Damn, what the hell. This can't be happening.* Hayden followed her to the blue checkered couch, and they sank onto the worn-out cushions.

"I'm glad you came, Hayden. There's something I need to tell you." She twisted her hands in her lap.

Hayden swallowed, his fear morphing to anger. "Yeah, I heard."

She scrunched her eyebrows. "What?"

Sitting next to her, smelling the strawberries floating from her hair, hearing her soft breaths before she prepared to deliver the death blow— Hayden want to shake her. How could she go back to Trevor after he'd told her he loved her? Didn't she care for him at all?

"How can you get back together with him? You didn't even give me a chance. You said I mattered to you. Or was that just a lie?" Hayden struggled to not yell at her. The unfairness burned a hole in his heart.

Molly narrowed her eyes. "What are you talking about?"

"Cindy told me you've been talking to Trevor again." Hayden stood and paced the stained carpet. "You could have at least called me after I told you I loved you, before you ran back to him."

Molly stood, too. Her hands clenched into fists at her sides. "First, you and Cindy shouldn't be talking about me. It's my business who I talk to."

Okay, she had a point. But his anger and hurt made that easy to ignore. She at least owed him an explanation. For crying out loud, he'd said I love you. He never even said it to his mother except for special occasions. He glared at Molly, waiting for her to finish.

She sucked in a breath through her nose and blew it out again. "Second, I'm not back with Trevor. I only talked to him to tell him I needed space."

Hayden stopped pacing. The rattle of the radiator hissed moist heat into the little room. They stared at each other for a moment. The anger in his chest dissipated with the steam and guilt wiggled in like a worm. He rubbed his eyes. "I'm sorry. I screwed up, didn't I?"

Molly crossed her arms, her eyes still narrow slits. "Yes, you did."

He opened his mouth to apologize again but could only stare at her.

Then she grinned. "It's a good thing I'm used to you acting like an idiot."

Hayden felt the tight knot in his chest loosen. He nodded in agreement. "I do, don't I?"

"Yes, a lot." She grabbed his hand and heat spread up his arm. Her grin faded. "But we have to talk about this."

The knot reformed. She sat back on the couch and pulled him next to her. Hayden rubbed her cheek.

She took a deep breath. "I've been thinking."

"That statement *never* leads to anything good." He tried to smile.

She sighed. "I know how you feel about me. And I have feelings for you, too."

"But…"

"But there's too much going on right now. I'm spread so thin I don't know who I am or what I want." She glanced at their hands.

He gripped hers harder to keep her from slipping further away. "Tell me what you need. I'll do anything for you."

The gap between them widened, and he tried desperately to hold on to the edge. Tears fell on her cheeks, and his hold got even more slippery.

"I need space. I need to figure out who I am, before I can know what I want."

The edge he gripped gave way, and Hayden went into a free fall. He spiraled out of control. "Molly, I can't stay away from you."

She wiped her eyes with the back of her hand. "I don't want you to. But I need you to be there as my friend. I can't give you more than that right now."

Hayden nodded. It could be worse. She could have told him she didn't want to hang out at all. "I'll always be your friend. And when you're ready for more, I'll be here for that, too."

She smiled. "You'll be the first to know if that happens."

Hayden didn't like the if. The if made his stomach twist. If didn't belong there.

"Don't get mad, but… what about Trevor?" She opened her mouth to answer. Hayden continued, speed talking to stop her from breaking his heart. "I know he says he wants you back. But it's only to keep you away from me. He doesn't care for you like I do." Hayden clenched his jaw, picturing Trevor with Molly.

"I don't know."

Those three little words jack hammered into his gut. They weren't a no for Trevor. Should he tell her Trevor cheated on her? That he told the guys lies about the things she did with him? He knew she would be hurt, but she'd understand how wrong Trevor was for her.

He wanted to tell her, to make her forget Trevor and say they were through. But he couldn't bring himself to cause her more pain. Instead, he settled with giving her a warning.

"I've known Trevor my whole life. He's said and done things you wouldn't believe." He chose his next words cautiously. "I don't want him to hurt you anymore, not when I was the one who brought you together. That wasn't supposed to happen."

"Don't worry. I hold Trevor responsible for his actions, not you. The space I need includes Trevor." She touched Hayden's cheek, and he closed his eyes. Her words didn't ease his fears. Hayden knew Trevor. He would be a total dick and hurt *her* just to hurt Hayden.

He bit his lip to stop himself from telling her everything. He nodded and leaned forward, bringing her hands to his forehead.

Molly pulled her hands away and wrapped him in a hug. He held her body to his, squeezing his eyes shut. He hid his pain with a smile before she let him go.

She wanted a friend. He wanted her. He'd waited this long, he'd have to wait a little longer. At least now she knew how he felt. It was worse before, watching her have a relationship with his best friend. Now at least he had a bit of hope.

Molly checked the clock. "You'd better go. My mom will be home soon, and you know her rule."

"Okay." He stood, and she walked him to the door.

She opened it and he turned to her.

"Molly, I'm patient but," his heart hammered in his chest. "Just know I'm ready, whenever you are."

She glanced at the floor then back to his eyes. "I'll see you tomorrow at school. I'm sure you've missed it."

"Oh yeah, can't wait to go back. See you tomorrow." He jogged down the steps and to his car. She watched from the door. He looked out the windshield of his Mustang at her sad smile.

Hayden waved as he pulled away, uttering words he'd never said before in his life.

"Yep, can't wait to go to school tomorrow."

CHAPTER ELEVEN

MOLLY

"You told Hayden *what*?" Cindy's raised voice carried across the parking lot. She glared at Molly. "You're crazy, girl. What is wrong with you?"

Walking toward the building, the crisp morning air blew in Molly's collar, sending goose bumps down her spine. "I told him I wanted to be friends." She shivered and held the door for Cindy. The school was warmer than outside, but the cold wind followed them through the opened door. They hurried toward their lockers.

Cindy grabbed her books and slammed the door shut with a bang. Several people jumped, glaring, then turned away when they saw it was Cindy. Her friend had a reputation for being a hothead. She tapped her foot and waited for Molly to gather her books. "You tick me off sometimes. You know?"

"I'm focusing on me. My mom suggested I take a break from the boyfriend issue, and she's right."

"Of course, she did, she's your mom. She doesn't *want* you to have a boyfriend." Cindy rolled her eyes. "My mom said I can't date until I'm out of college and have a job."

Molly giggled and closed her locker. They headed to their first hour English class. Molly's stomach filled with butterflies. How would Hayden act today? "I trust her. I need to figure out who I am without the influence of a boyfriend."

"Uh huh. And how did Hayden take the news?" They reached the classroom and stopped outside the door.

"He said he'd wait for me." She grinned remembering Hayden's words. "He said he would do anything I needed."

"That sounds like him. He's crazy about you, you know." Cindy grabbed the door to their class and pulled it open. "You better not make him wait too long. He might spontaneously combust."

Molly giggled, and they walked into the room.

Cindy dropped her bag by her chair with a thud. "Did Trevor get the same lecture?"

Molly frowned and took out her notebook and research notecards. "Yes. You were there when he called."

"Hmph. I thought you were letting him manipulate you again that night." Cindy smirked. "Was he understanding like Hayden? Did he say he would wait and do whatever you needed?"

Molly bit her lip and wrinkled her forehead.

Cindy touched her hand. "I know what that look means. What happened?"

Molly recalled the conversation and rubbed her temples with her fingertips. Trevor had called while she and Cindy studied for their math test. She'd answered the phone in a good mood, her head filled with thoughts of Hayden.

"Hello?"

"Molly, it's me." Trevor's voice chiseled away at her good mood. The last time they had spoken, he told her she was a lost cause.

"Hello, Trevor." Molly had met Cindy's gaze and frowned.

Cindy glared whispering, "Do not talk to that jerk."

But this phone call had to happen. She'd left the room so Cindy wouldn't hear.

"What do you want?"

"Before you hang up, please listen. I'm sorry, Molly. I didn't mean the things I said. I was just angry. And stupid. And selfish." He sighed into the phone.

Molly thought he sounded sincere, but he might be faking. He was an actor after all. "And?"

"I want to try again. I miss you, Molly. Can I come over, so we can talk?"

"No. My mom isn't home." Trevor knew the rules.

"When she gets back can I come?" His voice was a whisper. "I love you, Molly. Please give me another chance."

Despite her anger, she ached for his pain. She remembered the happy times they shared, the fun conversations, places he'd taken her. She missed that Trevor.

But that wasn't all of him. The snide remarks, the way he made her feel guilty for thinking of herself or anyone else besides him. That Trevor could suck it. She didn't want him.

"Trevor, I... I need space to figure things out."

"Space? From what? Molly, I can help you figure out anything you need."

She frowned into the phone. "No, I need to be alone to figure things out. For me."

His soft whisper grew harsher. "Does this space include Hayden? Is *he* allowed inside your space?"

"Space means space. From everyone. If you care about me, you'll wait for me."

"I'll wait. But not forever. That's not fair for me either. A relationship takes two people. Not just one who gets to decide everything."

After he'd hung up, she'd barely been able to study because of her anger.

In class, Molly sighed, her gaze meeting Cindy's. "Trevor reacted like you would expect."

Cindy chuckled. "Like a selfish bastard who thinks the world revolves around his asshole?"

Molly scrunched her nose. "Yes."

"Then I guess you have one thing figured out." Cindy leaned back in her seat, a huge smile on her face.

"Yes, I know for sure my best friend is biased and her opinion can't be trusted." She smiled at Cindy's wounded huff.

Movement at the door drew Molly's attention. Hayden walked in, his gaze immediately finding Molly. He smiled, and Molly's heart jumped in her chest. She ignored the whispers that sprung up around her as Hayden slid into his seat.

"Hey, girls. How are you doing today?" He winked at Cindy. "It's good to be back."

Cindy snorted. "I'd rather be home. Think if I punched Trevor I could get suspended for a few days?"

Molly laughed. "Sure, but then you wouldn't get to go to sectionals tomorrow."

Hayden turned to Molly. "Can I come watch?" He bounced his leg against the desk.

"I need my cheering section, don't I?"

He returned the smile and the bouncing stopped. "I'll be there."

"My mom is coming this time. She won't know how to see me on the course. Would you show her?"

Hayden's eyes regained the cocky sparkle. "Sure, tell her to wear running shoes."

Molly laughed and looked at Cindy.

Cindy watched them with a small smile on her lips. "Has your mom met Hayden?"

Shrugging Molly said, "No, but she's easy to get along with. I don't think she'll scare him too much. Now your mom on the other hand..."

Cindy and Molly laughed.

"Where should I meet her?" Hayden relaxed back in his seat.

It felt just like old times, before she knew he loved her. Hayden felt like her friend again. Molly's smile faded.

And it burned a lonely hole in her chest.

Without thinking, Molly reached for his hand. When they connected, he drew a sharp breath and she let go. She wasn't being fair to him.

She cleared her throat. "Well, why don't you meet her by the team tent. I run at 10:00 so get there by 9:30."

Hayden nodded. "Sure. That sounds good." He smiled again, the pain gone, or at least hidden.

"Mr. Bishop, I need to see you at my desk please." Mrs. Richter peered at Hayden over her glasses.

He looked at Molly. "Great, she probably wants to lecture me. As if three days of homework wasn't enough punishment. I'll be right back."

Once he'd left, Cindy grabbed her arm. "What the hell, Molly. You can't send mixed signals like that. That was just plain mean."

Molly's cheeks tingled. "I didn't mean to. He was being so nice and normal, and it made me feel sad. Like I was missing something. I didn't even know I did it until I touched him."

Cindy glared at her. "Well don't do it again unless you decide he's the one you want. Which, by the way, it's obvious he is. But I guess you need to figure that out for yourself." She leaned back and glared at the chalkboard.

Molly turned her gaze to Hayden standing at the teacher's desk. His spiked, dark hair was messy, his long-sleeved green rugby shirt hugged his broad shoulders. His acid washed jeans fit so snug against his thighs she could see the muscles flexing underneath while he shifted his weight on his feet.

She'd always thought he was cute, but he looked different today. Now, knowing he liked her, he looked... freaking hot.

"Shit," she whispered under her breath. She shouldn't be looking at Hayden. She should be focusing on her future.

Hayden turned and met her eyes. Molly swore he had an innate ability to catch her doing things she shouldn't be doing. Like checking out his body while he argued with the teacher.

He returned to his desk scowling and grabbed his backpack. Was he mad at her for touching him?

"Mrs. Richter says I can't sit here anymore. She thinks it would be better if I move away from you."

Relieved he wasn't mad at her, she mentally thanked their teacher. It might be better to put physical space between them. Maybe then she could concentrate on the mental space she needed to impose. "Sorry. Where do you have to sit?"

He snorted. "Next to Trevor. In the front where she can keep an eye on us."

Molly giggled. "Now I'm sorrier."

Hayden sighed. "I'll see you after class." He strutted to the front and took his new seat next to his new ex-best friend.

Remembering the way they used to joke and laugh with each other, her stomach squirmed. It was her fault they hated each other now.

Forget about them.

She gave her attention to Mrs. Richter's lesson on how to properly cite their research sources.

Focus.

Right.

Ignoring her brain, she sighed in defeat and her gaze drifted to Hayden's back. Her heart had other ideas.

CHAPTER TWELVE

HAYDEN

After school Friday, Hayden changed in the locker room. He put on his soccer shorts, practice jersey, and socks. Stuffing in his shin guards, he blew out a frustrated breath.

"Damn it," he mumbled to himself, trying to forget about Molly touching his hand in English. He'd wanted to grab hers, but he'd resisted because she said she didn't want that. Part of him wanted to give her space. Another part wanted to close that space and get a room.

He bumped the locker with his head trying, unsuccessfully, not to remember kissing her at his house.

"Hey, *Captain*. Welcome back to school."

Hayden stifled his groan. He didn't want to take any shit from Tim today. "Thanks." Hayden slipped his feet into his cleats and tied the laces.

Tim crossed his arms. "So, was she worth it?"

Hayden glared at Tim. "What the hell are you talking about?"

"Molly. You hooked up with her at Mike's party, right? Fucking your best friend's girlfriend? Not cool, Hayden. Was she worth losing your friend?"

Hayden jumped off the bench. "We didn't hook up. I took her home because she was wasted. And she isn't Trevor's girlfriend. They broke up *before* the party."

Hayden grabbed his bag and took a step toward the door. His emotions were out of control and this would get ugly fast.

Tim moved in front of him, blocking the way. "Yeah, right. Andrea told me she saw you coming out of the bedroom together. What were you doing in there, talking?"

It figures Andrea would stick her nose into this. Hayden narrowed his eyes at Tim's sneer.

"Yes, believe it or not, some of us aren't assholes and don't take advantage of drunk girls." Hayden stepped around Tim and toward the door. "Let's go. We have practice."

Hayden met the eyes of a few guys watching the discussion. They frowned, glancing between Tim and Hayden.

Tim grunted through clenched teeth. "I guess my sister wasn't good enough because she doesn't put out. Is that why you went after Molly instead? From what Trevor says she's a great lay."

Hayden jerked to a stop. Mike stood a few feet away, listening. He met Hayden's eyes and shook his head.

Hayden dropped his bag on the concrete floor. In three steps, he tackled Tim, slamming a fist into his mouth.

Tim groaned but swung back connecting with Hayden's left eye. They scuffled on the floor, throwing punches, Hayden landing a good one right into Tim's nose.

Mike and the rest of the team ran over to stop them. He grabbed Hayden by the arms while two others pushed back on his chest.

Tim lay on the floor, blood streaming over his red jersey and the floor. "Fuck you, Hayden. First your best friend now your teammate. You're just an asshole."

"If you talk about Molly like that, I'll kick your ass again. I don't care who you are." Hayden spit blood from his torn lip onto the floor next to Tim.

"What's going on in here?" The coach entered the locker room and the guys groaned. He glanced around, settling his gaze on Tim and Hayden's bloody faces. "Out on the field. Let's go."

The team headed toward the door.

"Bishop, Jones, in my office." The coach followed them, reaching into the small fridge on the floor then handing them two ice packs. Hayden covered his swelling eye and Tim held the pack on his nose.

"I'll pretend I didn't just walk in and see this." Coach glared at them. "Whatever beef you have with each other doesn't matter. What matters is we have a game against Altgeld Academy soon. We have *never* beaten them. This year we have a chance, but only if we work as a team."

He glanced between Hayden and Tim. "You'll both get suspended if I turn you in, and the team needs you. So, this didn't happen here, and it *won't* happen again. Understand?" Hayden and Tim both nodded.

Tim glared at Hayden and walked out of the locker room. Hayden stood to follow him.

"Hayden," Coach said, putting a hand on his arm. "What's going on? Two fights in one week?"

Hayden shrugged. "Sorry, Coach." He didn't know how to explain his lack of control.

Coach nodded. "If you need to talk, I'm here." He gestured to Hayden's swollen eye. "Can you practice?"

Hayden chuckled. "Sure, I still have one good eye."

Coach smirked, lowering his voice. "Well, Tim looked worse than you. I hope he deserved it at least."

Hayden remembered what Tim had said and wished the guys hadn't broken them up so soon. "He did, Coach. Totally."

"Tim can be obnoxious." The coach chuckled. "But he's a good soccer player. You both need to save the fighting for Altgeld. Come on, let's go."

Hayden followed the coach outside, guilt creeping into his stomach. It wasn't Tim's fault Trevor was an ass and had spread lies about Molly.

When Hayden got to the field, warm-ups had started. Tim sat on the bench holding tissues to his still bleeding nose. Hayden walked over, stopping in front of him.

They glared at each other for a moment, then Hayden shook his head.

"I'm not sorry for hitting you. You deserved it for what you said. Molly isn't like that, and neither am I."

Tim frowned, glancing at the guys running around the field. He looked back at Hayden and nodded. "Maybe it was out of line."

"But I am sorry, because you're right, we're teammates. We're supposed to have each other's backs." Hayden took a breath. "And I'm sorry about your sister. We didn't mesh, that's all."

Tim frowned. "She can be a bitch sometimes. I get it."

"And Trevor likes to spread lies. Molly hasn't done anything with him."

Tim shook his head. "She never seemed like the type, and everyone knows Trevor likes to run his mouth."

Hayden smirked. "You have no idea."

Tim stood and held out his hand. "I won't say shit about her anymore. I was just defending my sister."

Hayden shook his hand. He looked up at the team running around the field. "If we're cool, we better get out there."

Tim shook his head. "We're cool. You go, my nose is still bleeding. Maybe you should have been a boxer." He grinned and sat on the bench.

Hayden grunted. "I'll stick with using my feet. It hurts too much to use my face." He pointed to his swollen eye.

Tim laughed. Hayden did, too, then ran onto the field to join the rest of his team.

***

At home, Hayden parked in his spot by the curb and jumped out of his car. He grabbed his backpack and ran up the brick paved sidewalk to the ornate, dark-oak door of his house.

Smoke from the grill drifted from the back yard, making his mouth water. His dad barbequed any chance he got, which was fine with Hayden because his dad was a grill master. He even remembered his dad grilling on Christmas one time after shoveling away the snow.

Hayden threw his bag on the kitchen table and went through the sliding doors to the back patio. His dad wore a jacket and his grilling apron. He turned with a smile when Hayden closed the door. The smile evaporated when he pointed to Hayden's shiner.

"Again, Hayden? You mother's going to kill you." He turned to flip the burgers on the grill, then replaced the lid. He wiped his hands on his apron and gestured to the flowery cushioned patio chairs and glass top table.

Hayden sat, wincing at the cold fabric against his bare legs. He wished he'd put his warm-up pants on before he left school.

"Did you fight Trevor again?"

He knew his dad didn't like that Hayden had fought with his best friend's son. "No. Tim."

Hayden lifted his chin at his dad's frown. He wasn't sorry. Molly was worth it.

His dad sighed. "Hayden, you can't keep doing this."

"Dad, he deserved it, trust me. But we're cool. We both apologized."

His dad smirked. "That's nice. But it still doesn't excuse what happened. What did Tim do?"

Hayden paused. He didn't want to tell his dad the lies Trevor had spread about Molly. That was too much pressure for his dad, to keep that from his best friend. Instead, he told half of the story.

"Tim accused me of hooking up with Molly at Mike's house on Saturday and cheating with my best friend's girlfriend."

His dad raised his eyebrows. "Did you?"

Hayden knew his dad was just getting the facts. His inner lawyer always came out, even when he wasn't working a case. Still, it hurt that his dad thought he might do that.

"Of course not. Trevor had dumped her, and Molly was upset, and I took her home. Tim's sister Andrea told him lies because she was mad that I didn't want to go out with her. Tim said he was just defending his sister, and I told him I was defending Molly. We're good."

His dad stared, unblinking, into Hayden's eyes, one eyebrow raised. The same steady stare he'd seen his dad give defendants on the stand—and Hayden when he was in trouble.

Hayden stared right back with half the stare, one eye too puffy to use.

His dad nodded. "Well, I know that was only half the truth, but I hope it was at least the most important part."

Hayden smiled. He never could fool his dad. "Yes, sir."

"Are we ever going to get to meet this girl you keep fighting for?"

Hayden sighed, his grin changing to a scowl. "I don't know."

His dad tilted his head. "Why not? If you're willing to kick multiple asses for her, she must be important."

Hayden picked at the edge of the table. "She is, Dad. But I don't know how important *I* am to her. I've been friend zoned."

His dad grinned. "Ahh. I see. She and Trevor just broke up, eh?"

Hayden nodded.

"Then you need to give her time. Maybe she needs to regroup."

Hayden leaned back in the chair with his chin on his chest, picturing Molly's face. "She said she needed space to figure out who she is."

"Then it's a no-brainer, give her space." His dad patted him on the knee. "If there's one thing I know, girls are better than us at knowing what they need. Listen to her, don't try to fix things for her."

"I know. It's just hard." Hayden grimaced, kicking his foot into the leg of the table.

"And you're afraid she'll go back to Trevor."

Hayden clenched his fists.

"He's not right for her. He's doesn't respect her." Hayden met his dad's wise eyes. "She can't go back to him."

His dad stood and grabbed the spatula. "You can't make that decision for her. Be there for her, be her friend. If it works out, then you'll feel good knowing she's with you because you earned her, not because you made her feel guilty."

"Yeah, you just described Trevor's game plan. He'll lay the biggest guilt trip on her anyone has ever seen." Hayden held his head in his hands.

His dad touched his shoulder. "Then it won't last, and you can be there to help her pick up the pieces. Have patience. Anything good is worth waiting for." He reached for the grill and lifted the cover, releasing a cloud of burger scented smoke. "I'll talk to your mom. She won't bug you."

"Thanks." Hayden stood and turned toward the door. "I need to shower before dinner."

"Oh, Hayden?"

Hayden turned back to his dad and raised his brows. "Yeah?"

"Tell me, did Tim look worse than you?"

Hayden smiled, his eye closing from the pressure of his puffy lid. "Way worse."

His dad nodded, flipping the burgers one last time. "At least you got your point across."

Hayden laughed. He went in the warm house and headed for the shower. His dad may be a well-educated, successful lawyer, but he knew, sometimes, you needed something more than words to win.

CHAPTER THIRTEEN

MOLLY

The shrill chime of the alarm pierced Molly's ears. She slapped the clock and pulled the pillow over her head. She lay there, fighting the sleep still in her eyes until she remembered why she should get out of bed. Sectionals started in a couple hours.

Molly threw back the covers and jumped off her warm mattress. She ran across the hall to use the bathroom.

Her mom called out from the kitchen. "Good morning. I'm making breakfast, so hurry and get out here."

Molly smiled entering the matchbox sized kitchen, inhaling the smell of toasted bread, eggs, and sausage. Her mom stood at the stove, flipping eggs that sizzled in the pan.

"That smells great." She took her seat at the table and bit into a slice of toast. "Tastes great, too." She picked up her fork and cut off a bite of her egg.

"You need gas in the tank to make the motor run." Her mom joined her at the table to eat her own breakfast.

Molly laughed and ate her fuel. "Mom, Hayden will hang with you today and help you find me on the course." She finished the last of her eggs.

Her mom raised her eyebrows. "Hayden? I thought you were scaling back on the boys for now."

"He's just coming as a friend. I asked him to help show you where to go." Molly stood and carried her plate to the sink. She returned to her seat at the table.

Her mom frowned. "Do you think that's a good idea? If he likes you, won't this confuse you both?"

Molly swallowed and stared at the table. "I don't know. But I can't imagine not talking to him." She sighed. "Yesterday, he treated me like a friend, and it made me lonely. Maybe I do want to try."

Her mom chuckled. "It's your decision, but I'd give it time. You just broke up with Trevor. Don't rush into anything."

"I know. Hayden has been my friend for a long time. I don't want to lose that." She sighed and smiled. "Today I have other things to take care of, and I need to go get ready. I have to be at school in thirty minutes."

Her mom nodded, sipping her coffee. "Yes, I agree. Get a move on. You don't want to be late."

Molly went to her room to get dressed, considering her mom's question. Was hanging out with Hayden a good idea? The thought of not talking to Hayden made her stomach ache. Not an option.

Trevor was a different story. His words had hurt, and she was still mad at him. She wondered if he would come today and try to make up with her. He hadn't called her while he served his suspension.

Molly dressed in her uniform and warm-up suit. She threw on her slide sandals and grabbed her running shoes, then returned to the kitchen.

"Ready?" Her mom smiled.

"I'm ready. Let's go" The sun hung low in the cloudless blue sky. The air felt crisp and cool, and the wind was calm. A perfect day for running. She pictured the course and smiled. They walked to the beat-up old car.

Her mom said, "What a great day." She unlocked the door and climbed in, reaching over to pull up the other lock.

"It is. I can't wait to run." Molly buckled her seatbelt. "Hurry, Mom. I want to get there so I can warm-up."

Her mom turned the key and the engine sputtered to life. She gunned the gas to keep the car from stalling. "Here we go." She backed out of the driveway.

When they reached the school, she directed her mom on where to park then they walked toward the team tent next to the entrance to the cross-country trail. Molly greeted the few girls walking around the tent, yawning and stretching their legs.

Throwing her bag on the ground in the corner of the tent, she pulled out her shoes and slipped them on. She adjusted the tongue of each a few times and double knotted the laces, then stood and jumped around to make sure they felt right. She untied the right one and repeated the process until everything felt good.

Her mom watched the preparations with a smile. "Do you need salt to throw over your shoulder or a bulb of garlic to wear around your neck?"

Molly laughed. "Sorry, I've done this all season. I guess I'm superstitious." She hugged her mom. "I'm so glad you got to come today."

Her mom squeezed Molly's waist. "I am, too. I'd hate to miss such an important moment."

They hung out for a while, greeting the others. When Andrea walked in the tent, Molly turned her back.

Her mom eyed Andrea from across the tent. Smirking, she whispered, "I take it I won't meet her."

Molly snorted and looked over her shoulder.

"No, that's Andrea." She returned Andrea's glare. "She's a good runner, but she's never beat me. And it won't happen today either."

Her mom chuckled. "That's my girl."

She grinned at her mom but then Hayden entered the tent and her heart fluttered in her chest.

When Hayden found Molly, his shoulders straightened, and his lips curved into a smile.

Molly smiled back, then frowned at the purple shadow surrounding his left eye. She glanced sideways at her mom and caught the slight shake of her head and the knowing smile.

"Hayden?"

Molly's cheeks burned, and she nodded.

Hayden stopped next to her, winking and smiling his cocky grin. He mock punched her shoulder. "Ready to win?"

She slapped his arm. "Don't jinx me." She gestured to her mom. "Mom meet Hayden Bishop. Hayden, my mom, Lisa."

Hayden held out his hand. "Nice to meet you, Mrs. Mason."

Her mom smiled, her eyes flashing between them. She shook Hayden's hand. "Call me Lisa. I'm not that old-fashioned."

Hayden grinned. "Sure, Lisa."

"Um, who gave you that?" Molly pointed to his eye.

He laughed, his gaze dropping to the ground. "Well, it's a long story. Let's call it a soccer injury."

She nodded. "A soccer injury. Did you get hit with the ball?"

Hayden cleared his throat, shifting his weight from one foot to the other as he dropped his chin to his chest. "No, Tim accidentally hit me."

"Accidentally?" Molly said. "Must be some story."

He rubbed his nose and nodded.

The coach entered the tent and Molly pushed aside her questions. "Girls, time to warm-up. Let's get started." The other girls followed the coach.

Molly looked around the tent. "Wait, where's Cindy?" Her stomach tightened. "She's not here yet."

Hayden frowned. "That's weird."

Cindy ran into the tent. Her curly hair bounced around her face, falling out of the loose ponytail she'd made. Her uniform shirt was on inside out and her shoestrings flopped along the ground. "Hey, girl," she breathed to Molly. "I woke up late and my stupid car wouldn't start. My brother had to drop me off, and he refused to go further than the front of the building because it's so crowded. Idiot."

Molly laughed. "You should have called. My mom would have come to get you."

Her mom agreed. "She's right. And your shirt needs fixing."

Cindy ripped off her shirt. Hayden's eyes widened. He blushed and looked at his feet. Molly grinned, but Cindy didn't even glance his way. She flipped her shirt and shoved it back over her head to cover her sports bra. She bent to tie her shoes, then stood, smoothing her hair. "It's okay. I won't be winning anything today. I just want to be here when you do, Molly."

"You're worse than Hayden and my mom. Top five, that's it."

Cindy grabbed her hand like Molly was the late one. "Come on. Coach is waiting."

"Good luck, honey. Run fast." Her mom hugged her again.

"Thanks, Mom. I will." She looked at Hayden.

He nodded. "Good luck. Don't let Andrea sneak past you today."

She smiled and gave him a hug, leaning into his arms. "Don't worry, I won't." She stepped away, smiling, and followed Cindy out of the tent.

CHAPTER FOURTEEN

HAYDEN

"Show me the ropes, Hayden." Lisa smiled. "I haven't been to any meets here. Where should we go first?"

Hayden returned the smile, comparing Lisa to Molly. Her gray eyes had a few lines, her skin less smooth. But her warm smile lit up her face and made her youthful. The blond hair was the same, minus the blue streak.

He answered Lisa's question. "We can watch from the start line first. Then I know a few of the best places to wait for her." He gestured toward the door and followed Lisa out of the tent.

She squinted in the bright sunlight. "So how long have you known Molly?"

"Since last year when you moved here. We met during track."

Lisa tilted her head. "Oh, do you run?"

"Yes, I did the 4x4 and 4x100 relays." Hayden walked up to the roped off starting area where they had to stop.

"Why don't you run cross-country?" Lisa stepped up to the rope.

Hayden scanned the girls on the field until he saw Molly with her teammates. "I play soccer in the fall."

Lisa smiled. "I see."

They watched the girls while they completed their warm-up run outs. Hayden smiled at the concentration on Molly's face. This was a big day for her. His stomach knotted, and he took a breath to loosen it.

"Running has always been important to Molly." Lisa said.

"Yeah." Hayden glanced at Lisa. "She's a great runner."

Lisa nodded. "I'm proud of her. She's always done well at whatever she tries. But lately she's had trouble concentrating."

Hayden shifted his weight. "She has?"

"Yes. I worry because I'm not able to be there with my work schedule." Lisa blew out a breath and glanced sideways at him. "Thank you for taking care of her at that party."

Hayden straightened his shoulders, looking at Lisa. "She told you about that?" He hadn't told his dad because he didn't want to get Mike and Tony busted.

"She tells me almost everything. That's how I know I can trust her home alone for so long. I know she's responsible." She watched Molly high knee across the field. "But she wasn't that night, and I'm glad she had a friend who looked out for her."

Hayden's stomach twisted. Friend. He shoved his hands in his pockets and sighed. "I didn't want to see her get hurt."

Lisa smiled and touched Hayden's arm. "I can tell how much she means to you. She likes you, but she needs time to figure things out."

Hayden turned to face Lisa. "I'm trying to give her space."

Lisa nodded, her blond curls moving with the motion. "It's hard, I know. But if you care for her, you need to give her that space. When the time comes, be there for her, Hayden. Until then, let her figure things out."

Hayden frowned. "That's what my dad said, too." He kicked a stick from under his foot and watched it bounce through the wet grass.

Lisa laughed. "He sounds like someone I'd get along with. Especially if he's friendly like you." She turned her eyes back to

Molly. "Not many boys would listen to their friend's mom lecture them on how to woo her daughter."

Hayden laughed. "Well, my dad's a lawyer. I'm used to lectures."

"Listening is a good skill to have." Lisa waved to Molly across the field.

Hayden glanced back at Molly, remembering the softness of her arms when she hugged him in the tent. He wanted to do the right thing, but why did it have to be so hard? Why couldn't he kiss her and tell her she was being stupid, and that she belonged with him?

She smiled at him, waving while he gazed at her. He waved back, grinning. Her blond hair shone like gold in the sunshine. The high ponytail bobbed on the back of her head. Her strong, lean legs were pale under the black shorts of her uniform. A surge of longing squeezed his chest.

Molly looked away, leading her teammates in another run out. They ran for fifty yards then returned to the starting position.

The crackle of a microphone cut through the cool air and the announcer's voice blared through the static filled speakers. "Ladies, please complete your final run out and return to your places."

"Here we go." Lisa clapped. "I hope she does well."

"She will. She's a fighter." Hayden glanced at Lisa. "Are you ready to run? We need to get to the mile marker across the field before she does."

"I hope we're taking a shortcut?"

Hayden smiled and nodded. "Yes, we couldn't keep up with Molly."

The runners stood in a line across the wide starting area. Hayden wondered how many girls there were. Eighteen schools, one to however many girls per school, lots of competition. He looked to the stands, trying to figure out which ones were the college scouts.

The speakers crackled again. "Runners take your positions."

The huge mass of girls stood in their line, arms hanging, bending at the waist. Hayden checked Molly's face. She stared straight ahead, her jaw muscle twitched, her fingers flexed. She closed her eyes for a moment, took a deep breath, and blew it out.

Hayden admired her focus and determination. When she took the field, she was a different Molly than the girl he saw every day. This Molly knew who she was and what she wanted. He should tattoo the word *FINISH* on his forehead. Maybe then he'd win her over.

The speaker crackled. "On your marks, set…" Lisa and Hayden jumped at the pop of the gun. Molly dashed away from the starting line, mashed up with at least a hundred other girls. Hayden and Lisa screamed with the other spectators. Shouts of girl's names and team mascots went up into the air as the girls thundered past.

Hayden turned to Lisa. "Come on. We have a few minutes to get to mile one." He and Lisa trotted to the first viewing place and waited for Molly.

Lisa panted and looked back along the trail. "Come on Molly."

Hayden smiled and looked down the trail. "She'll be right behind the pace truck."

After four and a half minutes had gone by, the pace truck came around a curve in the woods and a lone runner came into view.

"It's Molly!" Lisa jumped and screamed. They watched her draw closer. They clapped and yelled her name. When she ran by, only her lips twitched. She was in the zone. Hayden knew how that felt. Like nothing could stop you, nothing could hurt you.

"Push it, Molly! You can do it!" Hayden yelled after her. He smiled at Lisa. "Come on, stop two is this way." They ran again. Lisa's ability to keep up impressed Hayden. "She must get her running talent from you. My mom would have collapsed if she were here."

"Well, waitressing takes lots of stamina." Lisa laughed.

They waited for the pace truck again. Molly was still in the lead, but she had someone closing in on her. Hayden wasn't surprised to see Andrea making her move.

"Keep your pace. Save it for the kick. She's catching up."

She darted her eyes at Hayden and winked. He chuckled. Molly wouldn't let Andrea get close enough to overtake the lead.

"Andrea is closing the gap." Lisa frowned.

"Don't worry. Molly knows what she's doing. And Andrea is already going all out. She'll run out of gas soon."

As Andrea ran past them, she panted hard. Her stomach heaved with her heavy breaths, her shoulders hunched forward with her effort to catch Molly. She stumbled on a stick and lost her pace, her groan of frustration cutting through the air.

Hayden almost felt bad for her. Then he remembered Andrea making fun of Molly and the pity evaporated.

"Where's the next stop?" Lisa asked.

"The next stop is the finish. And with the pace she has right now she might beat us there." Hayden laughed.

Lisa smiled and ran back to the field. "Let's go slow-poke. I don't want to miss this."

Hayden ran after her. They made it back with a minute to spare and stood together near the finish line. The pace truck came out of the tree line and pulled off to the side of the trail. The crowd cheered at Molly, the only runner in sight. She had a good lead on the field, but she ran like she had a knife-wielding maniac behind her.

Hayden laughed "She's trying to break the course record. I guess making the top five was too easy for her."

"What is the record?" Lisa's eyes sparkled in the sun. She clapped, watching her daughter approach.

"11:31." Hayden looked at the timer. "I think she's going to do it."

"Go, Molly. Dig, dig!" The coach screamed behind the finish line.

Molly increased her pace, legs pumping faster than Hayden had ever seen.

"You got it, Molly!" Lisa's cheeks were wet with tears.

Molly crashed across the tape and Hayden smiled. He looked at the clock, cheering at the 11:29 flashing on the screen.

The other girls left the trees and raced to the finish. Andrea followed next, crossing a full twenty seconds behind to get second. Hayden saw Cindy and yelled encouragement. She battled for fifth place.

"Go, Cindy! You can take her!" Hayden had never seen her finish this far up in the pack. She ran hard, arms pumping, legs flashing. She put her head down and gave one last effort to pass the other girl.

Cindy crossed inches in front of her competitor and Hayden and Lisa cheered. They ran over to congratulate both girls. Molly wrapped Cindy in a hug, squealing and jumping together as they celebrated.

"Omigod. You're going to state!" Molly grabbed her hands and pumped her arms.

Cindy laughed, her eyes filling with tears. "I can't believe it! I don't have to go watch this time! How about you? What was your time?"

Hayden answered Cindy's question. "11:29. She broke the course record."

Molly hugged her mom, and then hugged Hayden around his neck. He hugged her back, squeezing her waist and twirling her around.

"Put me down, you idiot!" She smirked, meeting his eyes. "Some things never change."

He raised his eyebrows. "Well, runners are superstitious. I don't want to break tradition and jinx you."

Molly laughed, her flushed cheeks and bright eyes were close. Hayden stepped back, so he didn't do anything stupid to ruin the moment.

The coach's voice interrupted them. "Molly come over here please." Only the U of I scout stood with the coach.

Molly's smile fell slightly. "I wonder where UCLA is."

Her mom rubbed her arm. "Go and talk. We'll be here when you're finished. Good luck."

Molly took a deep breath. "Thanks."

She glanced at Hayden and he smiled. "Go get your offer. You've earned it."

She rolled her eyes. "What was that you said about jinxing me?" She placed her trembling hand on Hayden's arm and squeezed. He patted her hand before she let go.

Hayden looked away. His stomach twisted, and he took a deep breath trying to ease his nerves.

Cindy laughed. "Hayden, you look like you're about to pass out. Relax, they'll want her."

He swallowed. "I know. I'm not nervous." He shoved his hands in his pockets, then pulled them back out and ran his hand through his hair.

Lisa patted his arm and smiled.

Cindy glanced across the field. "I need to go do a cool-down. I'll be back to see what they said." She jogged away.

Hayden shifted his weight between his feet. He kept his back to Molly and the scout.

Lisa glanced toward Molly. "She's smiling so it must be a good conversation."

He nodded. "I'm sure it is." He took another deep breath.

Lisa laughed. "Do you have plans after this? I thought I would take the girls out for a celebration lunch. Would you like to go with us?"

"Sure, but only if I can treat." Hayden smiled. "My dad would kill me if I didn't. He's old school, and I don't need another lecture."

Lisa shook her head. "Oh, you don't need to do that."

"I do. The last time I wasn't a 'gentleman' I got grounded and had to go with my mom to her book club and serve them tea." Hayden shuddered. "It was terrible."

Lisa laughed. "Your parents are a trip. I think I need to meet them sometime." Her gaze went to something behind him. The corners of her eyes tightened.

Someone tapped his shoulder and he turned.

"Hi, Hayden." Andrea smiled and glanced at Lisa.

"Hi." Hayden gestured to Lisa. "This is Molly's mom. Lisa, meet Andrea."

Lisa smiled, but it was polite, not warm. "Hello, Andrea. Congratulations. You ran a great race today."

Andrea's smile looked forced. She nodded and thanked Lisa. "Well, I PR'd, so I know I did all I could."

Hayden bit his lip. It had to suck knowing her best still wasn't enough to beat Molly.

Lisa nodded. "That's great. Good luck at state."

Andrea's shoulders stiffened. "Thanks."

Lisa nodded to Hayden. "I'll be over here waiting for Molly. Don't forget lunch." She took a few steps away from him and Andrea.

Andrea glanced at Hayden. "Are you going to Mike's tonight? He's having people over again." She reached over and brushed a piece of lint off his shoulder.

Hayden flinched. "I don't think so. I have other plans." He didn't, but he wasn't about to give her the chance to ask him out again.

She smiled and her dimples made her look friendly. Too bad she had the eyes of a snake. "Come on, it'll be fun." She touched his arm, leaning toward him.

Hayden shook his head. "We've already tried this. I don't want to go out with you." He brushed her hand away, glancing toward Molly. She still stood with her coach and the scout, her face impassive.

Andrea followed his gaze. Her eyes narrowed, and she lowered her voice. "She won't go out with you either I hear. Why bother, you know she's still hung up on Trevor."

Hayden glared at Andrea. "You don't know what you're talking about."

"Oh, I probably know more than you. Have a good *lunch*." She waved and walked away.

Hayden glared at her back, his brow creased. Her words left a pit in his stomach. Andrea loved to create drama and she could cause damage if she wanted to.

Molly's approach blasted Andrea from his mind. Lisa rejoined him, and they met Molly halfway.

Lisa grabbed Molly's hands. "So, what's the verdict?"

Hayden's heart beat in his throat.

Molly smiled. "He said he liked what he saw today. And if I can do well enough at state, they're prepared to make an offer for a full ride."

Lisa screamed and threw her arms around Molly. Hayden laughed, waiting for her mom to let her go. Then Hayden grabbed Molly and spun her until they were both dizzy.

"I know, I know," he said. "I'm an idiot." He set her on the ground, waiting for her to push him away. She didn't.

Instead she grabbed his face and kissed him. It was just a quick kiss but for Hayden time stopped.

"I haven't got the offer yet. I still need to run well at state."

Hayden laughed. "No problem. You always run well."

"Now I'll probably twist an ankle or something." Molly stepped back and slapped Hayden's arm, but her smile made the reprimand weightless. "Thanks for being here. But you are an idiot. I'm so dizzy, I'm not sure I can walk."

"Sorry." He gazed into her silver eyes with his heart about to burst from his chest like in the cartoons.

Lisa squeezed Molly's arm. "You better go do your cooldown. We're celebrating with pizza after the awards. Bring Cindy with you." She smiled and wiped her eyes. "I'm so proud of you."

Molly wiped her own tears. "Thanks, Mom. I hope the awards don't take long. I'm starving." She touched Hayden's arm then ran toward her teammates. Hayden smiled while he watched her jog away, taking his heart with her.

CHAPTER FIFTEEN

MOLLY

Sunday morning, Molly woke with Hayden's name on her lips. In her dream, they were kissing, a good dream by any standard.

She threw back the covers and crossed the hall to the bathroom. Her mom was still asleep, so she moved quietly, trying not to wake her. Her mom never got to sleep in, and Molly wanted her to enjoy the day off.

The shower worked on the first try and she giggled. "I guess my luck carried over into today."

She tapped her fingers on the counter, waiting for the water to warm. At the first hint of steam, she climbed in, her mind drifting to yesterday's events.

She was happy with the possible offer from U of I. Full ride. The golden ticket her mom called it. Too bad her first choice, UCLA, hadn't shown.

Her coach had explained after the cool-down. "He called. There was another runner in Iowa he had to scout. He wants to wait and see you at state to see how you handle the pressure." Coach Davis smiled. "I told him not to worry, you have a heart of steel and would perform great."

Turning off the shower, she dried, dressed, and went to the kitchen, hoping her coach was right. California's biology program, her chosen major, had a lot to offer. But maybe she'd have Chicago to fall back on.

In the kitchen, she mixed up pancakes, her favorite Sunday morning breakfast. Her mom used to make them when Molly was little, and the tradition continued once Molly became the cook.

She flipped the cakes onto a plate, setting aside a few for her mom. After slathering on the butter and syrup, she took a bite, remembering her dream. She pictured Hayden's face and her stomach quivered with longing.

She liked Hayden, that much was a given. But should she start a relationship with him now? What if they did, and she had to leave him for college? The scout had outlined the grueling practice schedule and time involved. Would it be fair to date Hayden now then push him aside for months out of the year while she trained?

Molly sighed and slid her plate away leaving the last few bites of pancake.

"Uh oh. Something wrong? I've never seen you leave a pancake stranded." Her mom grabbed a plate and buttered a pancake.

Molly smiled. "I was just thinking."

"About?"

"About Hayden."

Her mom nodded, chewing her first bite. "He's nice. I like him."

She grimaced. "So do I, Mom. That's the problem."

Her mom raised her brows. "Why? What's wrong with that?"

"Because, college will be hard. I don't want to start something with Hayden and not be able to finish it."

"What do you mean?"

Molly put her elbows on the table and leaned her chin on her hands. "What if I can't give him enough attention and it becomes a problem? That's why Trevor broke up with me. I don't want to do that to Hayden."

Her mom reached over. Molly placed her trembling hands into her mom's warm ones.

"You do what you think is right. But don't avoid a relationship because of something that *might* happen. There's a lot of reasons for relationships to fail. But the biggest one is a lack of communication. Talk to Hayden and see how he feels. If he's willing to try despite your commitment to running, then you should try, too."

Molly sighed. "You're right, Mom. I'll talk to him today." She wanted Hayden to say he would do anything for a chance to be with her, because she wanted him, too. She looked at the clock. "I wonder if he's up yet."

"Something tells me he won't mind waking up early on a Sunday for this conversation." The phone rang on the wall and her mom laughed. "Speak of the devil."

Molly rushed to the phone and lifted it to her ear, twisting the long cord between her fingers. "Hello?"

She waited for Hayden to greet her. Her stomach clenched when Trevor's voice answered instead.

"Hey, Molly."

She met her mom's raised brows. "Hi, Trevor. What do you want?"

Her mom shook her head and pointed to the bedroom. She left to give Molly privacy.

"Congratulations on winning sectionals yesterday," Trevor said. "That's totally awesome."

She squinted her eyes at the phone. Did he think it mattered what he thought?

"Thanks. It was awesome, not that you care. You didn't even bother to come and watch."

It didn't matter much to her if Trevor missed it because Hayden was the one she wanted to share that victory with, but she and Trevor had dated for over a year. He should have at least respected her enough to watch the most important race this year.

"Well, I wanted to come, Molly. I couldn't."

"Had something better to do?" She listened for Trevor's excuses to begin. In the background a voice over a loudspeaker paging someone, followed by loud beeping noises. Where the hell was he?

He chuckled. "You see, they won't let you leave the hospital right after surgery. They like to keep you and make sure everything is okay first."

Molly froze, her mouth open. "Hospital? Surgery? What are you talking about?"

His sigh echoed in her ear. "I'm at Mercy. I had surgery yesterday to repair my broken leg."

Molly's guilt created a pancake boulder in her stomach. "God, Trevor, I'm sorry. I didn't know." She rubbed her eyes. "What happened?"

Trevor cleared his throat. "Well, I'd rather not tell you over the phone. Can you come see me?"

"Uhm…" Molly pinched the bridge of her nose. "I'll see if my mom will let me use the car."

"Thanks." He paused. "I can't wait to see you. I miss you."

She hesitated, unsure what to say to his confession. "I'll be there soon."

"Bye. Oh, hey, wake me up if I'm asleep when you get here. They have me drugged up, and it's hard to stay awake. But I need to talk to you."

"Sure. See ya." She hung the receiver back on the cradle. Her mom came out from the bedroom.

"Everything okay?"

Molly shook her head. "Trevor's in the hospital. He had surgery yesterday on his leg and I need to go see him. Can I take the car?"

Her mom frowned. "Sure. Is he okay?"

"I don't know. I'm sure his leg will be okay, but he said he can't tell me more over the phone. Something else is going on." She bit her lip.

"Be careful. And tell Trevor I hope he gets better soon." Her mom tossed her the keys, giving her a serious look. "Remember, Molly, whatever happened to Trevor is not your fault. Don't let him guilt you into believing it is."

Molly frowned. "What makes you think he would do that?"

Her mom crossed her arms and lifted her chin. "Because, I've seen him do it to you before."

"I can worry for him without feeling guilty." But guilt had already settled in Molly's chest for snapping at him about missing the race.

"Yes, and I do hope he's okay." Her mom smiled. "Go. I'll see you when you get back."

Molly grabbed her purse and jogged to the car, trying not to think about Hayden and what she would rather do right now instead of going to visit her ex-boyfriend in the hospital.

She pulled into the parking lot twenty minutes later and entered through the main entrance. She stopped at the desk to get Trevor's room number, climbed the three flights, and followed the hall to his room. After a soft knock, she pushed the door open.

Trevor lay sleeping in the bed. She had expected to see the splint on his leg but gasped at the other injuries.

Bandages covered Trevor's head and neck and he had a brace on his right arm. His face sported two black eyes and swollen lips, with a neat row of stitches just under the lower one.

She stood in the doorway, unsure if she should wake him. He looked like he needed the rest. She took a step to leave and Trevor opened his bleary eyes.

"Molly, why didn't you wake me up? How long have you been here?"

She frowned. "I just got here. But I shouldn't be. You need rest." She put her hand on the door.

"No, please stay. I need to talk to you." Trevor tried to move and winced.

Molly rushed to help him. "Hold still. I'll stay, just don't move." She pulled a chair over to his bed. She sat, and he reached for her hand. She held it, looking at his bruised face. "Tell me what happened Trevor. Were you in an accident?"

Trevor groaned. "I wish. That might have hurt less."

"What happened?"

Trevor looked at his injured leg then closed his eyes. "Tim jumped me."

Molly gasped and covered her mouth with her free hand. "Tim? Why?"

Trevor nodded then winced again. "Well, he was talking, and I got mad at him. I told him to stop and he blew up." Trevor met Molly's eyes then looked away.

"What was he talking about?" Tim was huge, bigger than Trevor. Bigger even than Hayden. Why did Trevor antagonize him? Whatever Tim said, it must have been something bad.

Trevor sighed and gingerly touched his lip. "He was talking about you."

"Me?" She sat up straighter in her chair.

Trevor gazed into her eyes. "Yes."

"What was he saying?" She rubbed a shaky hand across her forehead.

Trevor shook his head. "I can't."

"Trevor, it's not fair for you to take a beating and not tell me why."

He bit his lip, closing his eyes for a moment. "Okay, but don't get mad at me for being the one to tell you."

Molly's pulse raced. "I promise. I won't"

Trevor took a breath. "He told me Hayden was telling everyone you two had sex at Mike's party last weekend. And it wasn't the first time either. Hayden said you'd been cheating with him."

Molly's blood froze. "That can't be true. Hayden wouldn't do that."

Trevor squeezed her hand. "That's not all. Hayden hooked up with Andrea. They've been doing it for a while. Tim and Hayden fought, too, at soccer. Hayden's just bigger than me and could handle it better." Trevor sighed. "When I told Tim it wasn't true and he'd better shut up, he got mad. He was so pissed about Andrea and Hayden I guess, and he has a temper. So, I had to take the beating for Hayden's big mouth."

Molly stared at Trevor's damaged face, remembering how Hayden had acted when she questioned him about his black eye. He'd said Tim hit him on accident. Her stomach ached. Trevor's story made more sense.

"Trevor, how do you know Hayden said any of this? Maybe Tim was lying."

"Molly, I hate to tell you but," he looked at their hands and back to her with tear-filled eyes. "Hayden told me the same thing. He was trying to get me to break up with you. I was stupid and believed him. Now I've lost you."

The tears fell on his cheeks and a hollow pit filled Molly's chest. How could Hayden do this? She covered her face, crying quietly.

"Please don't cry. It's not your fault." Trevor reached over to caress her hair.

She uncovered her face and met his eyes. "Trevor, I don't know what to say. I thought Hayden liked me. I never knew he could do this." She sniffed. "God, how could I be so stupid? I knew he was a player. I guess I got played."

Trevor brought her hand to his lips. "We both did. He was my best friend. I know how much this hurts." He smiled. "But, maybe now we can get back on track. I know I didn't always treat you right. Maybe things can be different. Maybe I can be different."

Molly swallowed her tears. "Let's try being friends again. Maybe things can move on from there."

Trevor smiled and touched her cheek. "Okay. I'd take any chance to spend time with you again."

His words stabbed her heart. They were the words she had hoped to hear from Hayden.

"I think I should go. You need to rest. I'll try to come back tomorrow after practice. Maybe Cindy will give me a ride."

Trevor smiled and closed his eyes. It took a second for them to open again. "I hope so. I'll see you tomorrow." His eyes closed again, and they stayed shut.

Molly walked to the door, pieces of her heart falling to the floor with her tears. When she opened it, and stepped into the hall, Hayden was there. He smiled that smile, like she was the best thing in the world. She pictured Trevor in the bed behind her, broken because of that smile.

Hayden reached for her and she pushed against his chest. She glared. "Don't touch me, asshole."

His eyes widened. "Molly, what's..."

"Don't ask me what's wrong. You know what you did. How could you? You're just a selfish prick."

Hayden gaped at her. Molly smirked. *Sure, now he has nothing to say.*

Tears blurred her vision. God, she had wanted him to be real. The pain from his betrayal drove deep into her heart, tearing it from her chest. She had to get out of there.

"Molly." Hayden shook his head and touched her arm. "I don't understand."

She ripped her arm from his grasp. "Just leave me alone. I never want to talk to you again."

Molly turned and ran to the stairs. She threw open the door and took the steps two at a time. In the car, she cranked the engine and peeled out of the lot, hoping her tears didn't blind her on the drive home.

CHAPTER SIXTEEN

HAYDEN

Hayden watched Molly run away, shock rooting him to the floor. Her words made no sense. What did she think he had done? Did she think he was the one who hurt Trevor? That was crazy. But she had *sounded* crazy.

He should chase her and figure out why she was so upset, but he knew he was too late. She'd already be at her car, leaving the lot by the time he could get there.

Instead, he entered Trevor's room. He'd bet anything Trevor was the one to blame for Molly's behavior. Shoving the door with both hands, he opened it and stepped inside.

Trevor laid on the bed, a giant smile on his face. He sat propped up on pillows with his hands behind his head. He turned and laughed when Hayden closed the door.

"Hey, Hayden. What's up?" Trevor greeted him like they were still ten, getting ready to ride bikes or play ball.

Hayden's stomach dropped. "What did you say to Molly?" He came after hearing Trevor had been hurt, and knew he should ask about Trevor's health, but he didn't care.

"Oh, that? Nothing much. I heard her yelling at you." He drew a breath between his teeth and shook his head. "Sorry, I bet that hurt."

Hayden clenched his teeth. "What the hell did you say, Trevor?"

"I told her how you were spreading nasty rumors about fucking her, Hayden. Tsk, tsk. That's not very gentlemanly of you. What would your mother say?" He narrowed his eyes. "Molly believed me since I defended her, and this is where I ended up. Poor Tim. My dad called in a few favors and now Tim's doing a little stint in juvie. Guess the team will need a new forward."

Hayden took a few steps toward Trevor and stopped, afraid to get too close and give himself the opportunity to add to the injuries.

"What happened to you? My dad said you got into a fight with Tim, but I know it wasn't because of Molly."

Trevor chuckled. "No, apparently, Tim is protective of his little sister. Too bad for him she's a slut. We hooked up a couple weeks ago, and now she won't leave me alone. She told Tim I used her, and he got pissed. He should learn to control his temper."

"Bastard. You couldn't just let Molly go. Why do you even care?"

Trevor glared. "Because, you always get what you want. Ever since we were kids, you always won. You always got the best position on the team, always got the praise for the win. Why do you think I asked Molly out in the first place? I could tell you wanted her. You would have won her too, but not this time. This time I get to see you lose."

He sighed, his smile returning, stretching his stitches until a small drop of blood appeared at the corner. "And do you know what? I like it."

Hayden's hands shook with the force of his anger. He backed toward the door, shaking his head. "There's something wrong with you." He had to get to Molly. He couldn't lose her because of Trevor's lies.

Trevor must have guessed his thoughts. He smiled. "She won't talk to you, Hayden. Not after she thinks you played her. I've covered my tracks. Tim is the only one who knows the truth and who is he going to tell?"

"He'll tell me. And I'll tell Molly."

Trevor laughed. It reminded Hayden of jokes they'd shared, good times in the past. How could Trevor change so much? Hayden felt a hollow pit in his stomach at the loss of his friend. But it didn't compare to the crater caused by losing Molly.

"Right, good luck with that. Let me know how things turn out." Trevor pushed the button on his pain pump and placed his hands back behind his head. "If you'll excuse me, I need to take a nap. Like Molly said, I need to rest so she and I can be friends again. She's coming to visit me tomorrow and I need to be ready."

Trevor scooted deeper into the bed, assuming a fragile, pained look. Tears pooled in his eyes. "I'm sorry, Hayden." His lip quivered, and he wiped his eye, wincing from 'pain'. Then he laughed. "Not."

Hayden fought the urge to hit him and walked out of the room ignoring Trevor's laughter. Once he fixed things with Molly,

Hayden would call the academy and recommend Trevor for the best actor award. He'd earned it.

***

Hayden drove to Molly's house. Her mom's car wasn't there but Cindy's sat in the driveway. He parked and ran to the door. After knocking, he bounced on his toes, eager for the door to open so he could tell Molly the truth.

When it opened, he held his breath. Cindy stood at the door, glaring.

"Get the hell out of here you lying bastard." She shoved his chest and Hayden stumbled backward.

"I need to talk to Molly," he pleaded with her. "You know I wouldn't say those things about her. Trevor's lying."

Cindy poked his chest with her finger.

"Right, I did my research. Several people have told me you said you hooked up with Molly while she was dating Trevor." She shook her head, making a disgusted noise with her throat. "And I thought you were better for her than Trevor. At least he didn't lie about her."

Hayden glared back, his anger rising. "I don't know who told you I said that, but they're lying, too. Trevor was the one who told guys he and Molly were having sex, not me." This couldn't be happening. It was like something out of a bad romance novel.

Cindy shook her head again. "You're something else, trying to turn this around and blame your best friend while he lays in the hospital because of what you said." Cindy moved to close the door and Hayden grabbed it.

"Cindy, please, let me talk to Molly. She has to hear the truth." Panic rose in his chest. Cindy had actually liked him. If she believed Trevor....

"No, she doesn't want to talk to you. And neither do I. Now let go of the door or I'm calling the cops."

Hayden stepped back, fighting the rising hopelessness. He stood on the porch, staring at the closed door.

What the hell was he going to do? How did you prove your innocence when you didn't get to take the stand? He didn't know, but maybe he knew somebody who did.

Hayden hopped off the porch and got in his car. He drove to the only place where he could find the truth.

CHAPTER SEVENTEEN

MOLLY

"I checked out Trevor's story," Cindy said, stomping through Molly's front door. She slammed it behind her and joined Molly on the couch. "Sorry, girl. I wanted Trevor to be lying, but he's not." She hugged Molly.

"I can't believe it. I thought Hayden loved me." Molly sobbed her pain onto Cindy's shoulder.

"Me, too. He had us both fooled." Cindy handed her a box of tissues and they sat on the couch. "I came prepared. Let's plot Hayden's death to make you feel better."

Molly sniffled, unable to work up a laugh. "Who did you talk to?"

Cindy rolled her eyes. "Everyone. Runners, soccer players, actors."

Molly's breath shook. "Who did Hayden say those things to?"

Cindy's eyes narrowed. "Well, the soccer players denied it, but they don't count because they're his friends. A few of the runners I talked to and Trevor's friends said they'd heard it, too. Some of them right from Hayden."

Molly's chin shook. She pressed the tissues to her eyes. "I was just about to tell him I'd go out with him. I thought he loved me, and I thought I loved him, too." She sobbed into the tissue. "Damn it, I do love him. How could he be such an ass?"

Cindy hugged her again. "You need to forget him. I know it's not easy, but you need to find something else to focus on. State is coming, and you can focus on that. I'll help you."

Even the thought of running didn't help Molly forget the pain. The sound of Hayden's voice as he argued with Cindy from the porch, ripped through Molly like a hurricane. She'd listened, biting her knuckle. If Cindy hadn't been there, she would have let Hayden in to lie to her.

"Damn, and he's a good liar" She waved to the door where Hayden had stood. "I almost believed him."

Molly glanced up from the couch. "Maybe I should give him a chance to explain."

Cindy frowned. "No, you need to stay away from him. Let me handle him for you. You'll believe anything he says because you want it to be true."

She groaned. Cindy was right. "Okay, but how am I going to avoid him at school tomorrow? Everyone will talk about me, too. God, this totally sucks." She flopped face first on the couch.

"I'll take care of that, too. Anyone talking about you has to deal with me."

Molly groaned into the cushion. "Maybe I'll just stay home."

"And miss practice? No way. You need to go there and show everyone you are stronger than the lies. And you are, Molly." Cindy smiled. "I got your back, girl."

"I know you do." Molly closed her eyes. Hayden's face floated up to tease her. She wanted him to be here, to hold her. She wanted him to not be an asshole who lied.

Cindy touched Molly's arm. "Do you want me to stay the night? My mom won't care."

"No, I want to be alone for a while." She sniffed and grabbed another tissue.

Cindy eyed her with narrowed lids. "You promise not to call him or let him come here?"

Molly nodded. "Yes, I'll sit here and wallow in misery by myself."

"While you wallow, eat ice cream. It will make you feel better." Cindy stood, frowning. "I'm so sorry. You don't deserve this. But you'll get through it."

Molly's eyes welled up again. She was tired of crying. "Thanks, I know I will."

She stood and hugged Cindy then closed the door after she left. Molly walked to her bedroom, throwing herself on the bed.

She sobbed on the pillow. Wallowing sucked.

***

At school on Monday, she sat with Cindy in English waiting for Hayden to enter. When he did, he walked right toward Molly. The pain on his face looked real.

Cindy stood in front of her and crossed her arms. "Stay away. She doesn't want to talk to you."

Hayden ignored her. "Molly come on, talk to me. You didn't even give me a chance to defend myself. You're just going to believe Trevor?"

Cindy glared at him.

Molly looked around the room. Other's had noticed the standoff. They stopped their conversations to watch the show. She whispered, "Cindy, sit. Everyone's staring."

Cindy sighed, but sat back in her chair. The hum of pre-class conversation picked back up.

Molly looked at Hayden, trying to ignore the stabbing pain in her chest. "She's right. I don't want to talk to you. There's nothing you could say to change my mind."

Hurt flared in his eyes. His eyebrows scrunched over his wild green eyes. "Not even the truth? Don't you want to hear that?" He sank into the seat in front of her.

She leaned back and crossed her arms. "I heard the truth, Hayden. It's your own fault if you don't like it. Maybe you shouldn't have lied and then I wouldn't have found out."

"I never lied about you." He stared into her eyes. "Why don't you believe me? Damn it. I didn't do this."

Molly trembled with the effort it took to stop herself from believing him. "Maybe you should have gone into acting instead of Trevor. You're better at it than he is." She looked away from the tears her words put in his eyes.

"Mr.Bishop take your seat so we can get started please." Mrs. Richter clicked her way across the front of the room.

Hayden blinked several times. "I'll prove I didn't do this."

She looked at her bag and pulled out her notebook. He walked away, and she bit her tongue to stop from calling him back. She wanted him so bad she almost didn't care what he'd said. What was wrong with her?

Molly stared at her desk for the rest of class, avoiding the stares, ignoring the whispers, and attempting to forget Hayden's tormented face.

CHAPTER EIGHTEEN

HAYDEN

Hayden's dad ran a hand through his salt-and-pepper hair, exhaling forcefully.

"You want me to give legal help to the kid who beat up and hospitalized my best friend's son?"

"Dad, Tim's never done anything like this before, and a first offense shouldn't have landed him in jail. You and I both know that." Hayden squinted his eyes. "Trevor said his dad had something to do with that."

Hayden knew his dad thought what Trevor did was total shit, but he didn't want to cause further strain with Trevor's dad. It was bad enough Hayden and Trevor had fought.

"Yes, he did. He pulled some legal strings, called in some favors." He looked at Hayden. "I don't agree with what he did, but I do understand. He's just looking out for his son."

Hayden snorted. "Yeah, as usual. Mr. Green always covers Trevor's mistakes."

Hayden stood from the armchair and paced his dad's office. The thick brown carpet muffled his steps.

His dad leaned back in his chair behind the huge cherry-wood desk. The worn leather creaked. "He does that a lot, doesn't he?"

Hayden shook his head. "Dad, can't you at least talk to the judge or something? Tim is a hothead and what he did was crap, but he was defending his sister. Besides, he's the only one who knows the truth, and can help me convince Molly that Trevor is lying."

It was a desperate plea, but Hayden was beyond desperate to make Molly believe him.

His dad sighed. "I'll talk to Tim, and I'll try to see what I can do. But I can't defend him, Hayden."

His dad tapped his fingers on the desk, chewing on his cheek. Hayden sensed his dad switch to lawyer mode.

"What makes you think Molly will believe Tim? Won't she think he was lying for you?"

"I don't know, Dad." Hayden rubbed his eyes. "I don't know what else to do. She won't talk to me, Cindy keeps threatening to beat me up, and I don't know where else to turn."

His dad rubbed his chin and pursed his lips, his lawyer thinking look. "Maybe, I can get a copy of the police record. They would have interviewed both boys at the time of the arrest. Have you asked Tim if he told the police why he beat Trevor?"

Hayden nodded, hope flaring in his chest. "Yes, he said he told them everything."

Molly and Cindy couldn't dispute an official report of the fight. Even if she still thought Hayden said those things, at least she would know Trevor was lying to her about the reason he and Tim fought. That might be enough to convince her to give Hayden a chance to defend himself. "Could you do that, Dad?"

He smiled. "Don't get your hopes up too much. I'll meet you there tomorrow after school and see what I can do. They might give me a copy. But if Tim has other legal representation, I won't even be able to look at his paperwork without contacting his lawyer."

"Thanks, Dad."

***

Hayden drove to the detention center after school the next day to meet with his dad and Tim. He walked up the steps and went inside. His dad stood at a gated counter, talking to a guard. He waved Hayden over, smiling at the guard.

"This is my son. Hayden, this is Anthony Rosario. We did our undergrad together at Northwestern."

Hayden smiled. If this guy was a friend of his dad's, they had a good shot of getting what they came for. Hayden stuck out his hand. "Nice to meet you, Mr. Rosario. I'll bet you have great stories about my dad in college."

Anthony laughed and shook his head. "I do, but your father wouldn't like me sharing those."

"Maybe I'll come back later," Hayden said with a grin. "You can tell me when Dad's not here."

Anthony smiled at Hayden's dad. "He's just like you, Jim. Knows how to smooth talk. He gonna be a lawyer, too?"

Hayden's dad laughed. "God, I hope not. If he does, he'd be a prosecutor. He's all about justice and fair play and making people pay for their crimes."

Hayden shook his head. "I think I'll choose an easier field, like horticulture."

Anthony glanced between them with a smile. "What brings you here today, Jim? You doing juvie law now?"

"No, I'm here to see one of Hayden's friends, Tim Jones. He came in here after a fight."

Anthony nodded. "Nice kid. I think his temper got the better of him. He's been good here. He should go to court next week. If he keeps cooperating, he should get a lighter sentence. It's his first offense."

Hayden's dad nodded. "I'm glad to hear it. Does he have representation yet?"

"No. I think he'll get a court appointed lawyer. Unless you want to help him out." Anthony raised his eyebrows.

Hayden smiled. Anthony probably thought his dad was here for that reason.

Hayden's dad shook his head. "No, but I'd like to look through his file and see if maybe there's anything I can do for him. I know a few juvie lawyers that might help."

Anthony nodded. "He's not eighteen yet. Did you talk to his parents?"

Hayden swallowed the lump in his throat. Crap. He hadn't thought of that. But his dad didn't miss a beat.

"Sure, they don't mind. They want him to get out of here and said they would take any help they could get." He pulled a paper out of his pocket and handed it to Anthony.

Anthony glanced at it and smiled. "Okay, I'll bring him to a visiting room, and you can talk while I get his file. You want a copy of the report to show your friends?"

For a second Hayden almost shouted yes, like Anthony was talking to him.

"Sure, that'd be great." His dad smiled. "Just leave out the stories about me. Hayden can think of his own ideas for college. I don't need him reliving any of our escapades."

Anthony's laugh echoed through the tiled entry surrounding the front desk. "You got it. I wouldn't want to see him end up in a place like this, not unless he was the lawyer."

Anthony buzzed them through the gate and led them into a room at the end of a long hallway.

After he left, Hayden smiled at his dad. "I didn't realize being a lawyer required the ability to lie so well."

"I didn't lie to him."

"Tim's parents know you're here talking to him?"

"Yes, I called them today to get permission."

Hayden shook his head. "What did you say to them?"

"That I was the father of one of Tim's teammates and would like to see if I could help with his case. I even faxed them the correct forms to sign." He pulled the papers out of his inside jacket pocket.

"I guess If I want to prove to Molly I'm not lying, I shouldn't expect you to lie for me." He patted his dad's shoulder. "Thanks for helping me. And Tim."

"Anytime someone is being falsely accused, it's an injustice. The truth will always win, and I like to be the one to help find it. Especially when my son is the one in trouble."

After talking with Tim, Hayden and his dad left the detention center. Hayden's dad said he could help find Tim a lawyer who might do work pro-bono. Tim's family didn't have a lot of extra money, and the court appointed lawyer would likely be overworked or inexperienced. With Hayden's dad's help, he would have a better chance of getting the lightest sentence of anger management classes and community service.

"I don't think Tim is a danger to society. Any decent lawyer could get him out of there." His dad clicked the remote entry for the door locks on his Nissan. Hayden wished his car had those. He still had to use a key.

He smirked at his dad. "Yeah, but Trevor's dad will push for the maximum. And Tim doesn't deserve that just because he can't afford a better lawyer."

"I'm glad you got what you needed Hayden. I don't think Molly will trust Trevor after seeing the report. Just don't lose it and don't let her keep it."

Hayden breathed deep and nodded. "I'll be careful with it. I don't want you to get into trouble."

"Thanks." He patted Hayden's shoulder. "Well, what are you waiting for? Aren't you going to go see her?"

Hayden laughed. "She's at cross-country practice now. I'll wait until later." He wanted to go when he knew Molly was alone, without Cindy there to convince her not to talk to him.

"Well, I'm going home. I'm taking advantage of this free afternoon to grill. I've got steaks in the fridge at home."

"See you later, Dad." Hayden sat in his car and watched his dad drive away. Then Hayden pulled out of the lot, driving away with the police report in his pocket and real hope in his heart.

CHAPTER NINETEEN

MOLLY

After practice, Molly had Cindy drive her to the hospital to see Trevor. They parked in the front lot and Cindy cut the engine.

"I hate hospitals. I'll stay in my car listening to my new cassette. I got *Brotherhood* yesterday and I can't stop listening to it. 'Every time I see you falling, I get down on my knees and I pray'." Cindy danced in the driver's seat.

"You're crazy. And the only black girl I know who likes New Order." Molly unbuckled her seatbelt and opened her door.

Cindy shrugged. "That's because I'm the only black girl you know. Do you plan on staying long? I have a lot of homework to do."

"No, only for a few minutes. I want to say hi and see how he's doing." She smiled at Cindy's doubtful expression. "I told Trevor yesterday I don't want to get back together with him. This is just a friend visit."

"Good, because both your options for men suck. You should wait until you go to U of I or UCLA. Maybe college men are more mature."

Cindy might be right. But as Molly crossed the lot and went into the building, she remembered Hayden holding her after sectionals. How excited he'd been for her win and her offer from the scout.

Walking up the stairs to Trevor's room, she mumbled, "Hayden's not what you need." Maybe not, but he was what she wanted.

Trevor was asleep again when she entered his room, so she walked to the chair. If he woke up, she would stay for a few minutes. If he didn't, she would leave and come back tomorrow.

The chair creaked with her weight and Trevor stirred in his bed.

He smiled. "God I'm glad to see you. I've been waiting all day for school to end."

Molly grinned. "Well, I had practice too. Cindy is waiting outside for me. I can't stay long. How are you today?"

"Tired of laying down." Trevor shifted in the bed and groaned. He tried to scoot further up the pillows. "Can you give me a hand? It's easier if someone helps."

"What should I do?"

"Just help lift my shoulders and push the pillows underneath." Trevor took a deep breath. "Ready when you are."

She put her arm behind Trevor's shoulders. She lifted him and pushed the white, bleach scented pillows under his back. Trevor relaxed on the bed and, at the same time, pulled her chest onto his, smiling. "Oops, sorry."

Sighing, she tried to pull away from him. "Trevor...."

"I know." His blue eyes had a mischievous twinkle. He squeezed her tighter. "Must be the painkillers. They make me forgetful."

He caressed her cheek and touched her lips with his finger. Molly pushed on his chest and this time he let go.

"Is there anything else you need? I have to go." Her stomach clenched.

Trevor wrinkled his brow and pushed out his bottom lip. "You just got here. Please don't leave yet."

Guilt gnawed at her stomach. It probably sucked to be here, and Trevor might need the company. She sat back in the chair. "Then behave yourself."

He grinned again. "I'll try. So, what's new at school?"

She shrugged. She didn't want to tell him how everyone watched her and talked about her. Or about Hayden's attempts to talk *to* her.

Trevor must have guessed though. He sighed. "Hayden's tried to tell you I'm lying hasn't he."

Molly nodded. "I don't want to talk about Hayden."

"Okay. Let's talk about us." Trevor drew his brows together. "Molly, I want you to come back."

"I'm not the one who left, Trevor." She crossed her legs.

"I know. Does that mean you still want to be with me?" His eyes widened.

"It means I can't come *back* to you. And no, I don't want to go out with you again. We're just friends remember?" Molly sighed and stood to leave. "Cindy is waiting, and I can see you want more than I can give."

"But, Molly, I love you. I made a mistake because I listened to Hayden. Don't make me pay for his lies. Tim already did that." Trevor gestured to his broken leg.

"I'm not *making you pay* for anything. I needed space before you got hurt. This doesn't change anything. There's too much drama right now and I need time alone to think things over. I'll only come back to visit again if you promise to be good."

She leaned and kissed his cheek. For a brief moment, she thought anger flashed in his eyes and she frowned. But then he smiled, and she ignored her imagination.

"I promise to be good. Please come, it's boring here. I can only stand so many crossword puzzles and TV game shows."

She laughed. "Okay, then I'll see you tomorrow. I'll bring a board game or something."

Trevor rolled his eyes. "That would be sooo much fun. Why not just shoot me instead?"

"Watch it or I'll bring Cindy. She'll find a way to entertain you."

Trevor shuddered. "No thanks, Monopoly sounds fine."

"Bye, Trev. I'll see you tomorrow." Molly smiled and left the room.

As she approached Cindy's car, bass vibrated the windows. Cindy bounced in the driver's seat, singing and dancing with the song. She looked up when Molly opened the door and slid into the car. She turned down the volume.

"That was fast. I thought you'd take longer." Cindy pulled out of the parking lot.

She snorted. "Yeah, well Trevor doesn't want to be friend zoned, and he's trying to make his move." She rubbed her eyes. "Maybe I shouldn't try to be friends. He doesn't want that, anyway."

Cindy signaled then turned onto Main Street. "Well, if he won't leave you alone then I agree, cut him off. You don't need any more boy issues."

"No, I don't." Molly stared out the window. Their little town flew past. The brick buildings on Main Street sat in neat rows.

Sometimes she imagined it was 1950 because these buildings had looked the same then. Red bricks, canvas awnings, the same white keystones above every window, like the designers ran out of imagination and replicated the same plans for each building.

Cindy took the turn for her street and Molly sighed. She needed to get home and chill. Forget about everything. But as they came closer to her house, her gut churned. Hayden's car sat in front of her house.

"Oh my God. Why is he here?" Molly's pulse spiked, beating in her eardrums.

Cindy groaned. "You stay in the car. I'll get him to leave."

Hayden stood next to his car, arms crossed, waiting for them. His face had lost the tortured look. His wide eyes and slight smile looked hopeful. Molly wanted to talk to him, but she knew Cindy wouldn't, and *shouldn't*, let her.

Cindy parked her car in the driveway. "Wait here." She opened her door and Hayden walked toward her.

"Get the hell out of here, Hayden. Why can't you leave her alone?" Hands on her hips, Cindy bobbed her head with each word.

"I have something that proves Trevor lied."

Molly's heart sped. Proof? What kind of proof?

Cindy cocked her head and crossed her arms. "Whatever lie you made up to blame Trevor won't work. Just go."

Molly got out of the car and closed the door. The heat from Hayden's stare melted the ice around her heart.

"Molly." He took a step toward her and Cindy shifted to block his path.

"Stay away from her. Molly, you go inside."

Hayden glared at Cindy. "Who are you, her mother? Molly, don't you want to talk to me?"

Yes, she screamed inside. But she shouldn't. He would just lie to her again. "No. I can't trust you." She clutched her bag so hard her fingers ached. "Please, go home."

"Do you really think I said those things?" Hayden reached around Cindy and touched Molly's arm. "I would never hurt you."

Cindy batted his hand away. "Go, Molly, and call the police. Maybe they can make him leave."

Hayden yelled at Cindy. "For crying out loud, Cindy. I'm not here to hurt anyone. I want to show you Trevor was lying. You used to be on my side remember? You never trusted Trevor. What did he do to change your mind?"

Cindy frowned, avoiding Hayden's eyes. Then she pulled back her shoulders.

"He told the truth." She turned to Molly. "Let's go." Cindy stalked toward the house.

Molly followed Cindy, then stopped and glanced back at Hayden, frozen on the driveway. The tortured look had returned to his face and planted seeds of doubt in her heart. Was she wrong? He seemed so sincere. Her insides felt like someone had put them through a shredder then blended them for good measure, creating one big soupy emotional stew.

He took a step toward her and she bolted into the house.

Cindy closed the door. "He's persistent, that's for sure. He must think we're stupid if he thinks we're gonna fall for his crap."

Molly rubbed her temples. "Have you considered that maybe Hayden is telling the truth?"

Cindy shook her head. "No, too many people told us the same thing. That many against one? Hayden's lying. Don't let your feelings for who you want him to be cover up who he is."

Everything was backwards. Cindy never went with the status quo, but this time she depended on the views of others to form her opinion of Hayden's guilt. Molly wondered why she was going along with Cindy, letting her control the situation. Were they both wrong?

What if they were? Hayden's question made sense. Cindy never trusted Trevor. Yet, now *he* was the one Cindy defended? Molly's head spun with indecision. She sighed and threw her bag on the table.

"I'm getting in the shower. Help yourself to whatever you can find. My mom said she'd bring home take out tonight before she had to go back to work." She escaped before Cindy could say anything else about Hayden.

In the bathroom, Molly tried to wash away the dirt, both from practice and from the way she treated Hayden. Instead, she pictured the look on his face and her tears joined the bubbles, trickling down the rusty drain.

CHAPTER TWENTY

HAYDEN

Hayden stood alone in the driveway. His hope lay smashed in the gravel under his feet like a piece of chewed gum. What good was the stupid proof if she wouldn't even give him the chance to show it to her.

"Fuck!" Hayden yelled at the top of his lungs. The neighbor sitting on his porch gave him a dirty look, then got up and went inside.

Hayden walked to his car and sat on the hood. He should leave. But he waited for...something. Something that could help him.

"Idiot. Nothing can help you now," Hayden mumbled to himself. This was his last hope, last idea. He pushed himself off the car.

Lisa pulled the Pontiac into the driveway. She stared at him through the window and Hayden couldn't decide if the look was friendly or not.

She parked and opened her door. Then she met his eyes.

Nope, not friendly at all. His stomach clenched. "You don't believe me either?"

Hayden could feel his control slipping. He wanted to cry, hit, run, anything to release the pressure. He settled for kicking his car tire, grimacing at the pain in his foot.

Lisa walked toward him, her graceful steps slow and steady. She furrowed her brow above her gray eyes, eyes like Molly's. "It doesn't matter if I believe you. Molly doesn't, and she's the one you hurt."

Hayden ground his teeth. "I didn't *do* anything. I never lied about her. Trevor was the one to spread the rumors. He told everyone he and Molly…" He swallowed. His fists shook with his pain and anger. "I love her, Lisa. I would never hurt her."

Lisa eyed him cautiously but not unkindly. "Why should Molly believe you? Trevor's in the hospital because he defended her—against lies he said you spread."

Hayden shook his head. "Tim didn't beat him up because of me. I have proof Trevor is lying."

Lisa raised her eyebrows. "This isn't a trial."

He threw his arms in the air and barked out a sarcastic laugh. All his anger and frustration exploded, and he yelled at Lisa.

"It sure feels like it. It feels like I'm the loser on The People's Court. Guilty with no chance of being proven innocent. I'm being prosecuted, but I'm not allowed to defend myself. Not one person has asked me for my side of the story." His shouts echoed off the house next door.

Lisa frowned then nodded. "Okay, you're right. You should have a chance to explain. What's your proof?"

Hayden unclenched his fists and reached into his pocket. He handed Lisa the police report.

Lisa took the paper. She read, and the crease between her eyes deepened. Tears gathered in her eyes. "Looks like you're right. Trevor lied to Molly."

Hayden sagged with relief. "And he lied about me, too. I never said those things about her, Lisa."

Lisa handed back the paper. "Have you shown this to Molly?"

"She won't talk to me. And Cindy is always there to pull her away." Hayden sat again, the metal hood creaking under his weight.

"Cindy is a great friend. She's always been there for Molly. But sometimes she can be overprotective." Lisa sat next to him and patted his knee. "I have to work tomorrow at both jobs. Normally, Cindy is the only one allowed here while I'm gone, but I'll make an exception. Come here tomorrow night when Molly is alone and talk to her."

Hayden blew out a sigh. "Thanks."

Lisa's light laughter took the edge off Hayden's hopelessness.

"I wouldn't lead with exhibit A either. She's smart. Give her a chance to believe you on her own. If that doesn't work, *then* show her the report."

Hayden rolled his head around his shoulders. "Right."

A movement at the window caught Hayden's eye. He looked but the curtain fell back into place. Was it Molly? He pictured her smile and the vise on his chest tightened.

Lisa sighed. "Go home, Hayden. I'll try to talk to her." She slid off his car and stepped up on the sidewalk.

"Thank you, Lisa." He opened the car door.

Her voice stopped him. "And, Hayden?"

He turned back to Lisa and raised his brows.

"I'm glad you didn't turn out to be the jerk I thought you were." She laughed, and Hayden could finally join her.

He waved and got into his car. Lisa went inside. Glancing at the empty window one more time, Hayden nodded. "Tomorrow, Molly. I won't leave until you talk to me."

At home, his dad was reading in the living room. He smiled when Hayden entered the room, then winced at Hayden's dejected face. "She didn't believe the report?"

Hayden fell into the armchair next to his dad. "She wouldn't even talk to me. She never gave me the chance to show her."

His dad set his book on the end table and sighed. "Are you sure this girl's the one for you? She doesn't sound very reasonable."

Hayden launched out of his chair and paced the room. "It's not her fault. Trevor has manipulated her since the day I introduced them to each other. Molly lets her friend tell her what to do because she doesn't know what to do for herself anymore. "And yes, she's the one, Dad. I love her."

He flopped back into his seat, covering his eyes with his hand.

"Then don't give up. What's the plan now?"

"Her mom told me to go there tomorrow after Cindy leaves and try to talk to Molly alone. So, that's what I'll do."

"Sounds like a good plan. Why is her mother helping you?"

"Because she *is* reasonable. She read the report and now she believes me." Hayden huffed a laugh and laid his head on the back of the chair. "You two might be the only ones though."

His dad picked up his book. "I don't know, Trevor knows you didn't do it. He believes you."

Hayden laughed. "Okay, I guess that makes three of you." He stood again, stretching his arms above his head. "I'm going to my room to do homework and go to bed. Good night, Dad."

"See you tomorrow. I'm sure it will be a better day."

"Sure."

Hayden bounced his bag onto the bed and tossed his shirt next to the hamper. His pants and shoes made it to the doorway of his bathroom. He turned on the shower and stood under the warm spray.

"What a fucking disaster." He let the water hit his face, trying to wash away memories of her. But Molly bubbled up in his head, refusing to go away. Hayden had no choice but to let her in.

CHAPTER TWENTY-ONE

MOLLY

"Cindy, can you take me to the hospital again?" Molly grabbed her bag then slammed her locker. "I told Trevor I would come again today." She sighed and slung her bag over her shoulder.

Cindy raised an eyebrow. "If you don't want to, then don't go."

They walked out of the locker room to Cindy's car. She shook her head. "It's not that I don't want to go." She kicked a stone and watched it skitter across the gravel parking lot.

Cindy opened the car, and they threw their bags in the back seat. Cindy slid into the driver's seat. "Then why do you look like your Walkman ran out of batteries and your Swatch fell in the toilet?"

Molly laid her head back on the seat and closed her eyes. "I don't know."

But she did know. She wanted to talk to Hayden and hear his proof but was too afraid to listen to herself. Would she ever be able to make her own decisions? She made a different excuse. "I'm just tired and want to get home to veg out."

Cindy turned the key. "Let's get this over with then." They drove out of the school lot and through town.

Cindy rolled to a stop at a red light. "I should get home early tonight, anyway. My mom has a special dinner planned. She's on this Huxtable kick and thinks we need to eat dinner as a family every night. At the freaking table. She even expects us to talk to each other about our day." Cindy rolled her eyes. "I think she's going through a midlife crisis or something."

Molly laughed. "Maybe it's just PMS."

"TV dinners and eating in separate rooms used to be fine with her. Not anymore. Now we act like the freaking Brady Bunch or something. Well, if the Brady's had had four boys and a girl and no Alice to clean up after them."

The hospital lot teemed with cars. Cindy found an empty spot in the last row. "Want me to come up with you? Trevor won't want me there, maybe you can get out faster."

She smiled at her omniscient friend. "Would you?"

"Only if I get to push the button on the elevator."

"I usually take the stairs."

"Okay, then we race, and you let me win."

"You're on. Let's go."

They crossed the lot and entered through the main doors. Running to the stairwell, Cindy pushed Molly back at the bottom step and she laughed. On the top step, Cindy shouted, "Yes," pumping her hands in the air.

"Goofball." Molly pushed open the door to Trevor's floor. As they drew closer, she heard laughter, loud laughter, coming from Trevor's room.

Cindy glanced at Molly. "Sounds like we're late to the party. I thought you said he could barely stay awake." She reached for the door, but Molly stopped her.

"Wait." She listened at the door. Trevor's laugh boomed out again and this time she heard his father's voice.

"Trevor, sit before you break your other leg."

"Just a minute, Dad. I can't stand being in bed anymore. One more lap."

Cindy raised her eyebrows. "Lap?"

Molly frowned and narrowed her eyes. "Wait out here."

Cindy nodded, and Molly pushed the door open. She stopped just inside the room, crossing her arms over her chest.

Trevor hopped around the room on his good leg, smiling, no trace of weariness or pain. His unbandaged head bobbed while he jumped away from the bed. The pale green hospital gown flapped around his legs. He froze when he saw her standing in his room. The smile disappeared. He wobbled and grabbed the edge of the bed.

His dad smiled at Molly. "Hi, Molly. I'm glad you came to visit this daredevil. Maybe you can get him to stop acting like a kangaroo."

She raised an eyebrow. "I see you're feeling better, Trevor." She smiled at his dad. "Sorry, Mr. Green. At least he's awake today. I'm sure he's ready to get out of bed after not being able to stay awake the last couple days."

His dad tapped the arm of his chair, smirking at his son. "Trevor, have you been lying to Molly?"

Molly held her breath, staring at Trevor while he sat back on the bed. She squeezed her hands into fists under her arms.

"Of course not, Dad." Trevor sighed and pulled the white blankets over his legs. His gaze bounced everywhere except for Molly's eyes.

"What do you mean, Mr. Green?" Molly swallowed and clenched her teeth.

Mr. Green laughed. "I mean, he's been out of bed for a couple days. But I'll bet he's been milking the sympathy from you for attention. Don't let him get away with that. He'll have you doing everything for him if you don't watch out."

"Thanks, Dad. Don't you need to go? I thought you and Mom were going to dinner."

His dad looked at his watch. "Yes, I'd better get going. I don't want your mom to get upset." He pushed out of the chair and patted Trevor's shoulder. "Behave yourself and quit acting like an invalid. I'll be back in the morning to bring you home. Good-bye, Molly. Sure I'll see you around the house."

"Good-bye, Mr. Green." *I'm sure you won't.*

He left the room and she glared at Trevor.

"I didn't lie… I just wanted… I mean I was hurt but I might have played it up some." Trevor groaned and flopped his head on the pillow. "It wasn't lying."

Molly stood between the bed and the door. "How was it not lying? You acted like you couldn't move yesterday. I had to lift you so you could sit up in bed."

A blush spread across Trevor's cheeks. He narrowed his eyes. "Well, maybe it was the only way I thought you would care. Sometimes I feel like you don't."

Unbelievable. He hadn't changed. He was blaming her for his lies and trying to make her feel guilty. Her mom was right.

A disgusted hiss left her mouth. "This isn't my fault. You're the one who lied."

He raised his head, the redness spreading to his neck. "But you're the one who made me *have* to. Maybe if you showed me you cared I wouldn't need to pretend I was hurt more just to get your attention."

Molly opened her mouth and stared at him. He didn't apologize or even act like he'd done anything wrong. That was bullshit. And she was done.

"I'm leaving. Don't bother calling me again because I'm finished with this. I'm tired of you blaming me for things I didn't do." She turned toward the door.

Trevor laughed, and she turned back around. His cold blue gaze chilled her blood.

"Whatever, Molly. I'm sure Hayden would take you back. Oh, but wait, he lied, too. Maybe it's because *you* don't know how to have a relationship and you force guys to make shit up. You're too selfish and don't think about us." He leaned back in the bed and sneered.

The hot sting of tears covered her eyes. She ran out the door. Cindy sat on a bench in the alcove across the hall. She clenched her jaw.

"Now what did he do?" She took a step toward Trevor's room.

Molly grabbed her arm. "Just take me home."

Sighing, Cindy placed an arm around Molly's shoulders. "Okay, come on."

As they drove home, Molly stared out the window. Was Trevor right? Did Hayden lie because she didn't think about his feelings? Because she didn't consider his needs? She wiped another tear from her cheek.

Cindy parked in Molly's driveway and cleared her throat. "I'm sorry. I was wrong. I thought Trevor might have changed or at least was trying to be less obnoxious."

"It's not your fault. He's good at manipulating people." They pulled into the driveway and Molly hugged her. "Thanks for the ride."

"You going to be okay? You could come eat dinner with us and be the youngest one in curls." Cindy tugged on Molly's blond ponytail.

She blinked away more tears. "No thanks. I need to chill for a while. I want to be alone."

Cindy grunted. "Yeah. I'll see you tomorrow."

CHAPTER TWENTY-TWO

MOLLY

Molly locked the door. Her mom wouldn't be home until late, and with Cindy gone, she grabbed a book to help her relax and forget her problems. Sure. Like that could ever happen.

Maybe hot water will help.

She showered, then went to the kitchen and pulled a frozen pizza from the refrigerator. She flipped on the TV while she waited for the oven to heat. Wheel of Fortune blared from the speaker. She grimaced and turned the knob to a different channel.

A loud knock echoed from the door and she jumped. It was late, and she wasn't expecting anyone. She crept to the window overlooking the porch and peeked out, cringing at Hayden's car in the driveway.

"Shit. Now what?" She dropped the curtain and hid behind the door. She shouldn't open it. If she ignored him, he'd go away. She could do that.

He knocked again. And again. Molly pretended not to notice the knocks getting louder. On the fourth and loudest hammer, he spoke.

"Molly, I know you're in there. I can hear you moving, and I smell the oven. So, unless you open the door, I'll assume your house is burning and you're tied up and I need to bust open the door to save you. Which means I'll get hurt or your neighbors will call the cops and I'll be arrested and my dad will ground me for the rest of my life."

Molly stifled a smile. She didn't want to smile at Hayden. He didn't deserve it. Then she thought about Trevor. He didn't deserve for her to be friendly either after the way he treated her, but she'd given him a second chance.

"Please, Molly?" Hayden's muffled request squeezed her battered heart.

She leaned her forehead against the door, and imagined Hayden doing the same. She hunched her shoulders. Cindy would kill her, but it was time to hear Hayden's side of the story. She opened the door, peering with one eye at his face.

He leaned against the frame and gave her a small smile. "I'm glad you opened it. I don't know how to break down a door."

Molly bit her bottom lip and held the door open. Hayden stepped inside, and she closed it behind him.

"Thanks for letting me in." His hands twitched like he wanted to touch her.

Molly's heart sped when she thought about letting him. "Why are you here?"

He gestured to the couch. "Can we sit?"

She pulled out the kitchen chair. The couch was too comfortable, and he hadn't earned that. Hayden sat in her mom's chair and she took her seat across the table. He continued to look at her, hands laying on the chipped yellow surface.

Molly put hers on her lap. "So? Talk."

"I'm not sure where to start." He lifted one hand and pinched the bridge of his nose.

Molly narrowed her eyes. "Why don't you start by telling me the truth?"

"I *have* been telling you the truth. I never said those terrible things."

She gazed at the fading bruise around his eye. "Tell me about Tim. When I asked you where your black eye came from, you never told me."

Hayden frowned. "I did. I told you Tim hit me."

"You never said why he hit you. You said it was an accident." She crossed her arms and waited.

"The reason I didn't tell you was because I didn't want to hurt you. And by not telling you, I hurt us both." Hayden shook his head. He met Molly's sardonic stare. "I was in the locker room and Tim asked me if you were worth losing my friend for. He said Andrea told him we had sex at Mike's party."

Molly wrinkled her forehead. "So, why did he hit you?"

Hayden looked her in the eye. "Because I hit him first. Tim asked if I didn't like his sister because she didn't "put out" and if I dumped her to go for you because you did. He said Trevor bragged you were good. That's when I jumped on him to shut him up."

She squinted. "That sounds like Trevor's story, only he was the one fighting and you were the liar."

Hayden leaned toward her. "Molly, you know me. Do you think I would do that?"

She didn't answer. "But why didn't you tell me that's what happened?"

Hayden closed his eyes. "I didn't want to tell you Trevor had been saying those things about you because I knew it would upset you."

Molly considered Hayden's story. It made sense. The way Hayden described everything, the personalities did what she expected. Trevor's story had seemed so far-fetched, so unreal. But she couldn't trust herself to believe Hayden any more than she could Trevor.

She looked into Hayden's emerald eyes. "So, Tim didn't hit you because you had sex with Andrea?"

Hayden scoffed. "Hell no, I never had sex with Andrea. We went to a movie and she spent so much time gossiping, I never asked her out again. I don't even know what happened in the movie. And it was a good one, too." Hayden shook his head.

Instead of clearing things up, the conversation made her more confused. "Trevor told me that Tim beat him up because of you. Tim said you used Andrea then me, and when Trevor tried to make Tim stop talking about me, he beat Trevor and put him in the hospital.

Trevor said he was defending me because you had spread lies about me sleeping around."

Hayden listened to her with his eyebrows traveling further and further up his head. "And you believed him?"

Molly crossed her arms. "Well, he was lying in a hospital bed bandaged from head to toe and in a lot of pain. He had more proof than you do right now."

Hayden grunted. "I have proof if you want it, but I'd rather try and convince you without it."

She glared. "Why? Isn't it real?"

"Oh, it's real." Hayden surprised her by grabbing her hands. Molly gasped but didn't pull away. "It would mean more to have you believe me because you trust me."

She held her breath. Her instincts were screaming to believe him, but her head told her not to. Nothing made sense. "I'm so confused."

Hayden squeezed her hands. The warm pressure sent butterflies into her throat. Molly swallowed them.

"Trevor said he got beat up because he was defending you?"

"That's what he said." Even to her ears it sounded ridiculous.

Hayden released her hands and reached into his pocket. He tossed a folded piece of paper on the table and leaned back in his chair. "That's my proof."

She wanted to believe him without it. She wanted to throw the paper in the trash and kiss Hayden right there in her dingy run-down kitchen. But too much pain stood in the way, like a cinderblock wall.

She picked up the paper and unfolded it. "What is this?"

Hayden leaned his elbows on the table. "It's the police report from Trevor and Tim's fight."

Molly's eyes widened. "How did you get this?"

Hayden raised one eyebrow. "My dad's a lawyer."

She looked back at the paper and read the arresting officer's notes. Trevor's signature followed the record of his version. She read the whole thing, twice. Molly's face grew hot and a hammer pounded behind her right eye.

It was all there. The truth. Trevor lied about everything, which meant he probably lied about Hayden. The upside-down world flipped back into place. Her heart had tried telling her Hayden was innocent, but Cindy, the others, even she herself, had convinced her of the opposite. She and Hayden had gone through hell because of Trevor.

With shame burning in her stomach, Molly admitted it was because of her, too. She was such an idiot for relying on others to tell her what to believe and listening to them without giving Hayden a chance. Trevor had manipulated her. Again. And she had hurt Hayden because she didn't make her own decisions.

Looks like I'm the idiot.

She moved to the living room and slumped on the couch. Hayden stayed at the table bouncing his knee and biting his lower lip.

When Molly leaned forward and held her head in her hands, Hayden joined her, sitting on the edge of the cushion. She raised her head and the tears fell on her cheeks.

"Don't be mad at me. I thought this would show you Trevor was lying. That if you knew he had lied about his fight with Tim, then you might believe me when I said he lied to you about me." Hayden's eyes brightened with tears. "That you would believe me when I told you I love you and I didn't…"

Molly wrapped her arms around his neck. A sob tore from her throat. Hayden buried his face in her hair and held her.

"Hayden—" The rest of her sentence caught in her throat.

Hayden breathed in her ear. "Does this mean you do believe me?"

She nodded, squeezing his neck.

He sighed, pulling her closer. "Dammit, Molly. I've missed you so much." Hayden kissed her neck then held her again. "You really believe me?"

She pulled back and nodded, wiping her eyes. "Why did so many people say you told them I had sex with you?"

Hayden touched her cheek. "Who said that?"

She thought about the kids Cindy talked to. The theater kids. Trevor's friends.

"God, I was so stupid. It was Trevor's friends and some girls on our team. I'll bet they were Andrea's friends." Molly leaned her forehead on her hand. "Cindy even said the soccer guys defended you, but we couldn't trust them because they were your friends."

Hayden pulled her hand away from her face and held it in his. "Molly, you're an idiot."

She smiled. "Takes one to know one."

"Can't argue with that logic."

She leaned onto Hayden's chest. He kissed the top of her head and rubbed her arms. His touch was better than ice cream at chasing away the sadness.

She raised her head. "I can't believe Trevor could be this cruel."

"I think he's just messed up." Hayden leaned back on the couch and pulled Molly's head onto his shoulder. "But he is a great actor."

She wrapped her arms around his waist and snuggled closer. The muscles in her back relaxed and the headache melted away. She snorted. "No kidding. John Hughes could use him in his next movie."

Hayden leaned his cheek on her head. "They could call it, The Bait and Switch Club. Trevor could have the lead role."

Molly put her hand on Hayden's chest, and he played with her fingers. Her heart raced with his body pressed so close to hers.

"If I ask you something will you be honest with me?"

He covered her hand with his. "That's the lesson I've learned from this mess. I'll never hide anything from you again. Unless it's your birthday present."

Molly's stomach jittered. Maybe she shouldn't ask. She wasn't sure she wanted to know the truth.

Hayden pressed her. "What did you want to ask me?"

"Never mind." She snuggled deeper into his chest.

Hayden pushed her away to see her face. "Come on. Talk to me."

Molly stared into his eyes, enjoying again the familiar swooping sensation in her stomach. "You're right. My mom said communication is the most important thing in a relationship."

"Smart lady." He raised his eyebrows.

Molly closed her eyes and sighed. "I was wondering if you've ever…" She whispered the rest of her question. "Done it."

His silence filled the room. Molly's gut twisted. She tried not to hate the mystery girl who he'd been with. She opened her eyes to his smile.

"No, I haven't."

She opened her mouth in surprise.

"What?" Hayden tickled her. "Did you think I was that kind of guy?"

She giggled. "You have gone out with almost every girl I know."

"Wow, just because a guy goes on dates doesn't mean he's a gigolo. I'm not David Lee Roth." Hayden shook his head.

Molly kissed his cheek. "I'll take that song off your soundtrack."

"You have a soundtrack for me?" Hayden rubbed his fingers through the blue streak in her hair.

"Yes." Molly smiled. "Cindy started it. She said I was your *Jessie's Girl.*"

"Accurate. What else?" Hayden's emerald eyes glowed under his dark lashes. His touch left a trail of goose bumps on her arm.

"This morning I would have added the *Policy of Truth* by Depeche Mode. But I think it's safe to take that one off the list."

She slid her hands up Hayden's chest. The thin fabric of his t-shirt left little between her fingers and him.

His muscles flexed under her touch and he drew in a shaky breath. "And what do you want to replace it with?"

She smiled, leaning in closer. Her lips hovered over his. "I think *Lovesong* by the Cure, don't you?" Her lower lip brushed against his.

"I agree." Hayden caressed her face with his fingers. His hoarse whisper floated between them. "Can I add a song to the list?"

Molly couldn't answer with her heart in her throat. She nodded.

Hayden traced the side of her neck with his fingertips. "I think we need a little Echo, because you definitely have *Lips Like Sugar*."

Hayden reached behind her neck and pulled her lips to his. Rubbing her back, he slipped his hands under her shirt to the soft skin of her waist beneath.

Tremors tickled up her spine and she pressed herself to his chest. She pulled her fingers through his silky hair, from the spikes on top to the longer hair in the back.

Her head spun as his warm hands moved over her skin. Or maybe that was from too much blood racing through her body. When he rubbed her waist again, Molly thought her head would explode. She moaned.

Hayden pulled back. "Sorry, I shouldn't do that. I don't want your mom to kick me out now that you've let me back in."

Molly's blood boiled under her skin. She swallowed to wet her throat. "She knows you're here?"

He grinned. "She told me it was okay to come talk to you after Cindy left for the night."

Molly rolled her eyes. "That figures. No wonder she told me to give you a chance. Trevor sealed the deal though. I caught him in a different lie." She described the scene at the hospital and what Trevor had said.

"What an asshole. But his lie worked in my favor." He scooted back on the couch.

She leaned against him, inhaling his fresh clean scent.

Hayden slipped his arms around her waist. His chin rested on her shoulder. "I told you I could treat you better. Will you let me now?"

He kissed her earlobe. Shivers radiated along her neck and shoulder.

"Well, let me think," she teased. He nipped her ear and she jumped with a squeal. "Hey!"

"I was just seeing if you tasted as good as you looked." He pulled her back to his chest. "I love you," he whispered, his breath warm on her ear.

She frowned. "I don't know if you should say that to me."

"Why not? It's how I feel."

Molly turned to face him. "But what if I can't say it back?"

He tucked her hair behind her ears. "You like me. Right?"

"Considering I'm making out with you on my couch I'd say that's a given."

He chuckled. "Then that's enough. It beats having you ignoring me and running away when I get too close."

Molly remembered Trevor's parting words. Was she bad at relationships? Shouldn't she tell Hayden she loved him if he was brave enough to tell her?

"What is it?"

She traced his bottom lip with her finger. "Am I selfish?"

Hayden frowned. "Why would you think that?"

That wasn't a no. Her heart thudded. "Am I?"

"You're *not selfish*. Trevor treated you like crap and conditioned you to feel guilty." He kissed away the frown on her lips. "I want you to love me, too. But you can say it when you're ready."

Molly wiped the tears from her cheeks. "Thanks."

"I have a serious question for you, though."

"What?"

His stomach growled. "Think the oven's ready yet?"

He winked, and Molly giggled. She stood and pulled him off the couch.

"Sure. Come on, I'll share my pizza with you."

"See. I told you you're not selfish." He caught her by the waist and kissed her neck, traveling up to her chin and landing on her lips. "Thank you for trusting me. I hated being without you."

"Me, too. I'm sorry for hurting you."

"I guess I didn't ask." He squeezed her to his chest. "Will you go out with me, Molly?"

His smile warmed his eyes until they glowed like new grass in the spring sunshine.

Molly pretended to think about it, and Hayden raised his eyebrows.

Then she smiled and kissed his lips. "Yes, I will."

He spun her around in the kitchen like she'd just won a race. "Yes, thank you!"

She laughed. "Put me down you idiot."

"Yes, ma'am." Hayden set her feet on the floor. "But I'm never letting you go again." He sealed the promise with a kiss.

CHAPTER TWENTY-THREE

HAYDEN

Hayden pulled into Molly's driveway the next morning and smiled—the same smile he'd worn since last night.

He left his car running and jogged up to the door. Lisa walked out, digging in her purse. She wore the blue polo shirt uniform from her factory job.

She looked up, keys jangling in her hand, and grinned at Hayden. "Good morning. Nice to see you here again."

Hayden nodded. "Thanks, it feels nice too."

"Molly is in the kitchen. Go on inside." She patted his shoulder. "I'm glad it worked out. Be good to her."

"Don't worry. I will." Hayden glanced at his feet. "She's important to me."

"I know." She winked a silver eye and walked to her car.

Inside, Molly sat at the table eating breakfast, reading her history book. She looked up when Hayden entered. Her cheeks flushed, and she rushed over to hug him.

He kissed her cheek. "Good morning."

"What kind of hello is that?" She held his face and kissed his lips.

Hayden held her hips and pulled her closer. "That's a way better hello than mine." He kissed the tip of her nose. "Are you ready for school?"

Molly rolled her eyes. "No, I want to stay here with you. Trevor will be there today you know."

He rubbed his hands along her back. "Don't worry. I'll be there with you." Hayden took her hand and picked up her bag. "Come on, let's go. I can't wait to show you off."

"Excuse me?" She playfully poked his chest as they walked outside. "What do you think I am, a trophy?"

"No, it's just this week has sucked. Today will be more fun." They walked through the sunshine to his car. The inside was warm and felt nice compared to the chilly morning.

He kissed her then backed out of the driveway. "I want people to know we're together and to know you know I wasn't a two-faced liar."

Molly laughed, the sound filling the car. "That's a lot of knowing."

Hayden wiggled his eyebrows. "I know."

She groaned and rolled her eyes.

In the parking lot at school, Hayden reached for Molly's hand. Her smile trembled, and he kissed her fingers. "Ready?"

She nodded, and they walked into the school. Several sets of eyes bulged. Hayden heard the whispered exclamations follow them to Molly's locker, like air hissing out of a balloon.

Molly grouched. "Geeze. Can't they stare at something else?" She opened her locker and yanked out her books.

Hayden reached over to brush his fingers along her hair. "I don't know, maybe we should give them something to stare at." He smiled, and Molly snorted.

"Right and let everyone think Andrea and Trevor were telling the truth." She closed her locker and slung her bag on her shoulder.

Hayden sighed and shook his head. "I don't care what anyone else thinks. Your opinion is the only one that counts." He put his hands on her hips.

Molly slid her arms around his neck. "I didn't know you had such a corny side."

He tickled her sides and she giggled.

"I'm not corny, I'm romantic. And you're mean. But I knew that about you." He kissed her cheek.

She pushed him away. "I'm not mean, I just don't put up with your idiocy. I'm trying to help you grow out of it."

"You're doing a fine job, too. I feel smarter already. Come on, let's go to my locker before class." He held her hand again while they walked.

Hayden strode toward English with his chin held high, eager to see the look on Trevor's face when he and Molly walked in together.

When they crossed the threshold, Trevor's red-faced glare made Hayden want to moonwalk across the classroom. Too bad he didn't know how. Hayden squeezed Molly's trembling hand.

"Trevor looks pissed." To spare Molly's feelings, Hayden tried to keep the excitement out of his whisper.

But she smiled. "Serves him right. That's what he gets for being an asshole." Trevor tried to catch her eye. She turned her head from Trevor and pulled Hayden to her seat.

Hayden tried not to laugh. "Remind me to never make you mad."

"Oh, I'm not mad at Trevor anymore. And I'm sure I'll get mad at you sometime because you act like an idiot, remember?"

Hayden opened his mouth to argue, and she put her finger on his lips. His heart sped like it always did when she touched him, but it was more satisfying because he knew Trevor was watching. Hayden tried to bite her finger, but she pulled it away, giggling.

"Hey. I don't always act like an idiot, do I?" He held up his hand. "Maybe you shouldn't answer that question."

Molly shook her head. "Only sometimes. But that's okay, it's cute." She ran a finger down his face. Hayden swallowed. She moved her soft fingers to his hands and Hayden took a deep breath. If she kept touching him, they might star in a show that could get them both suspended.

Hayden cleared his throat. "Where's Cindy?"

Molly looked away from his eyes. "I called her last night. She said she'd be late today because she had a dentist appointment."

Hayden touched the frown line on her forehead. "She still doesn't believe me, does she?"

"She does, but she thinks I rushed into this relationship. Which makes no sense because she was the one trying to push us together before this whole mess started."

Hayden shrugged. "Does it matter to you? What Cindy thinks?" His mind had been on Molly for so long nothing felt rushed, just the opposite—long overdue.

She rubbed her fingers along his arm. "She's my best friend. I always care about her. But, this time she's wrong."

He agreed.

Mrs. Richter's voice cut into their conversation. "Everyone take your seats. We have a lot to get through today." She eyed Hayden and he saluted her.

Molly patted his shoulder. "You'd better go. Good luck. At least I don't have to sit by Trevor."

He chuckled. "See you after class." He squeezed her hand then walked to his seat. Crutches leaned against Hayden's chair. He put his bag on the floor and grabbed the sticks. "Where do you want these, Trevor?"

"You can shove them up your ass, Hayden."

He smiled at the venom in Trevor's voice. "I'll put them over here for you. They won't do you much good if I take your suggestion." He leaned the crutches against the wall nearest to Trevor's desk.

Trevor glared at him. "Fuck off. What did you do, Hayden?"

Hayden frowned. "What?"

Trevor's face reddened, and he dropped his voice to a harsh whisper. "You told her what I did, didn't you?"

"No." Hayden thought of the police report. "You told her on your own."

Trevor squinted, opening his mouth to reply, but Mrs. Richter started her lecture, cutting him off.

Hayden frowned, glancing at Trevor from the corner of his eye. He remembered when he and Trevor had fun together—ball games, Saturday afternoon roller skating at the rink. Those days were long gone.

But Hayden would choose a relationship with Molly over friendship with Trevor any day. She was worth it. Hayden leaned back in his seat, a grin on his face, Molly's kiss in his thoughts, and his old best friend stewing beside him.

CHAPTER TWENTY-FOUR

MOLLY

Molly rushed from her stats class to meet Hayden waiting for her at lunch. She lifted her bag higher onto her shoulder and pushed her way into the crowded hall.

"Molly."

Dread filled her empty stomach. Trevor leaned against the wall outside her room, holding both crutches under one arm. He grabbed her elbow when she came through the door.

"Let go of me." She pulled her arm from his grasp. "I don't want to talk to you."

Trevor glared. "But you'll talk to Hayden?"

Molly narrowed her eyes. Students passed by, bumping into her while she argued with Trevor. She could step closer to him and avoid the crowd, but she'd rather be jostled than allow Trevor to touch her.

"I have to go." She took a step, trying to walk past him.

Trevor grabbed her again, this time he held tight. He curled his lip. "Come on. You could at least talk to me. You owe me that much."

Molly glared at him. "Are you kidding me? You lied about Hayden, you lied about me, and you lied about Andrea." She leaned closer and lowered her voice to a snarl. "You had sex with her while we were going out. I owe you *nothing*."

"Hayden told you, didn't he? He's lying. He wants you to be mad at me instead of him." He shook his head, his narrowed eyes glittering with anger. "And you're stupid enough to believe him."

Molly's face burned with heat. She glanced around at the students walking near them. Some of them watched her and Trevor, smirking or just listening in with curious expressions. She straightened her back and put her hands on her hips.

"If you want to do this here, fine." She smiled and raised her voice. "Hayden wasn't the one who told me you had sex with Andrea. You did. I read the police report from your fight with Tim where you admitted everything."

Trevor's face paled. He glanced at the others. "What are you talking about?"

"You know what I mean. Tim didn't beat you up because of me. He kicked your ass because you used his little sister. You made up the story about Hayden, so I wouldn't go out with him. Hayden never told people we did it, because we haven't. You spread those rumors, too." Angry tears filled her eyes. "It's over, Trevor. I'm not listening to you anymore. You're a cheat and a liar and I'm *smart* enough to know I don't deserve that. Hayden treats me better. He shows me respect, something you've never had for me."

Trevor blushed, red seeping down his neck. "I…" He swallowed. His gaze darted to the giggling onlookers. He met Molly's eyes and glared. "Fine. We're done."

Molly rolled her eyes. "Good-bye, Trevor. Leave us alone." She spun on her heel and strode through the hall, chin held high, ignoring the stares and whispers.

***

In the cafeteria, Molly met Cindy at their usual table by the wall filled with windows. The weak autumn sunlight flooded in, warming the hard, plastic seat where she sat. She laid her head on the table and groaned.

"Rough morning?" Cindy laughed, eating her slice of pizza. She took a sip of milk and continued. "Maybe you should have stayed home today."

Molly raised her head. "I wanted to. My mom said I had to face the masses and show them that I knew what I wanted."

Cindy folded her hands on the table and looked down her nose at Molly. "And what is that? Have you figured it out yet?"

Hayden walked through the door catching Molly's eye. When her heart did a somersault, she answered Cindy's question with a definitive, "Yes." She smiled at him and he hurried toward their table.

Cindy followed her gaze and snorted. "I told you, girl."

"You were right. Now be nice."

Cindy raised her eyebrows and tucked her chin. "Hey, he's the one who has to be nice. You don't need another guy who treats you like garbage."

"He won't. Trust me." Molly sighed when Hayden reached their table.

Hayden placed his tray on the table and sat next to Molly. "Hello, ladies." He kissed Molly's cheek and nodded to Cindy.

Cindy raised an eyebrow. "You have another chance to prove yourself. But I'm watching you."

Hayden glanced at Molly. He cleared his throat then held Cindy's hand between his. Her shoulders snapped back, and her eyes widened.

"Cindy, I never lied to Molly, and I won't ever lie to you. I love her, and I promise to never hurt her. I'll be there for her like you always are. You have my word." He delivered his deep-voiced, husky promise with a fiery intense gaze.

Molly looked at Cindy and pressed her lips together to smother the smile. Cindy stared at Hayden, her mouth opening and closing like a fish.

Hayden winked at Molly. "How was that?"

She laughed and patted his arm. "Corny, with a capital C." He nodded, a satisfied smile on his face.

Cindy snatched her hand away from Hayden and laughed with Molly. "Damn, maybe you should have gone into acting,

Hayden. You could have the lead role in any romance with those lines." She fanned herself.

Hayden took a bite of his pizza and shook his head. "Nah, then I'd have to hang out with them." He jerked his chin to Trevor and his friends who watched Hayden with angry glares. "You never know when they're lying and when they're telling the truth. That's why they're actors. I'll stick to soccer."

Cindy pursed her lips. "You ain't wrong about the lying." She leaned closer to Molly. "I've heard talk."

Molly's laughing mood vanished. She sighed and glanced at Trevor's table. "What now?"

"Well, Andrea's been telling people her brother is in jail for beating Trevor because Hayden told Tim she and Trevor were having sex."

Molly clenched her jaw and pushed away her tray. "They did, Cindy. Trevor admitted it in the police report."

Hayden put his hand on Molly's. "I never told Tim. When I saw him at juvie, he said Andrea told him about Trevor." He picked up his milk and took a drink.

Cindy crossed her arms. "Well, Andrea says it's not true because she's a virgin. Hell, if *she's* a virgin then I'm the Mother Mary. That girl's been with more guys than a porn star."

Hayden coughed, and milk sprayed onto the table. Molly laughed and threw a napkin at him.

He wiped the milk, smiling. "How do you know anything about porn stars?"

Cindy shrugged. "I have a twin brother and I pay attention when people talk. That's how I heard what I'm telling you now."

Molly found Andrea across the cafeteria, sitting by Trevor. She laughed at something he said and rubbed her shoulder against his.

"Well, she's perfect for Trevor then." She smiled at Hayden.

Hayden smiled back. "I agree, they make such a cute couple. But Tim might have something to say about it."

Cindy looked at the clock then collected her bag. "Just be careful with that little ho, Molly. She has something up her skinny little sleeve."

Molly sighed. "I'm sure you're right." Why was Andrea such a pain?

After they finished, Hayden took the trays back to the rack.

Cindy grabbed Molly's arm. "I'm serious. Andrea's been whispering something about you. I don't trust her."

Molly's stomach clenched. "I'll be careful. But I'm not afraid of her, Cindy." She giggled. "If nothing else, I can always out-run her."

"That's true." Cindy looked behind Molly. "I don't want to be the third wheel. I'll see you in gym." Cindy waved and hustled away.

Hayden slipped his arms around her from behind. He kissed her cheek and rested his head on her shoulder. "Ready to go? The bell's about to ring."

Molly turned in his arms and hugged him, listening to the sound of his heart beating under her ear. She smiled when it beat faster.

"Lunch was too short." She grabbed his hand and walked toward the double doors leading to the crowded hall.

Hayden walked with her to the locker room. He sighed when they reached the door. "Do you want to hang out after practice today? I'll be finished around 3:30." He rubbed her palm with his fingertips.

Molly's breath caught in her throat. "Sure, but my mom has to work. Can we go somewhere?"

"Let's go to my house." He grinned at her gasp. "You can eat dinner with us."

"O-kay." She looked at the floor. "Are you sure I should meet your family? Your dad is friends with Trevor's, right? Won't he be mad?"

Hayden lifted her chin with his finger. "No, that doesn't matter to them. And it wouldn't matter to me if it did." Hayden kissed her. "I love you, and so will they."

Tears gathered in Molly's eyes. She tightened her grip on Hayden's hands. The words I love you, too danced on her tongue, but fear froze them to the roof of her mouth.

"You aren't supposed to cry when I say I love you." Hayden grinned.

Molly sniffled. "Cindy was right. You should be a leading man. Definitely swoonworthy."

"You're the only one I want swooning." He glanced at the clock. "We'd better go. You don't want to be late for gym."

Molly groaned. "No, I'd hate to miss aerobics. That's way more fun than standing here with my boyfriend whispering romantic lines in my ear." He laughed, and she reached up on her tip toes to kiss him. "I'll see you after practice."

"Okay, I'll drive to the course to pick you up." He squeezed her hand and walked toward his class.

In the locker room, Molly changed and threw her things in the locker. Jumping around like Jane Fonda didn't go well with a full bladder so, she headed for the bathroom. When she left the stall, she held back a groan.

Andrea stood at the sink fixing her hair. She glared at Molly in the mirror. "Well, look who's here. It's miss superstar. How's it feel to win every race and still finish last?"

Molly ignored her and walked to the sink to wash her hands.

"Aren't you even going to answer? Or do you still think you've won?" Andrea's lip curled while she glanced over Molly's body. "You know Hayden's just using you to get back at Trevor."

Molly grit her teeth. "Shut up, Andrea. I know the truth. Trevor's yours now. Leave me and Hayden alone. She turned to walk away.

Andrea blocked her path. "I don't want Trevor." She pushed Molly in the chest.

Molly stumbled back a step. "What the hell, Andrea. What's the matter with you?"

Andrea pushed her again. This time Molly fell backwards and leaned on the sink.

Andrea sneered. "Aren't you going to fight back? Oh, that's right, you might get suspended and you don't want to miss state. Gotta get that scholarship."

Molly righted herself and glared at Andrea. She took a step again to walk around her.

Andrea reached out and grabbed the sleeve of Molly's shirt, slapping at Molly's face. Molly blocked Andrea's hands and struggled to push her away. "Stop it, Andrea. This is ridiculous."

"Fuck you, Molly!" Andrea screamed. She raked her nails across Molly's arm. Molly cried out, using her free arm to block Andrea's fist before it connected with her face.

Feet pounded as girls ran through the locker room, their sneakers squealing on the tiled floor. Girls flooded the door to the bathroom, gasping when they saw Molly and Andrea.

Someone grabbed Andrea from behind and flung her to the floor. Cindy. She jumped on top of Andrea, throwing punches. Andrea screamed at Cindy to stop. Girls exclamations and shouts echoed off the tiled walls and concrete floor.

Andrea bucked, trying to knock Cindy off her.

"You crazy bitch." Cindy yelled at Andrea. "You want a fight, I'll give you one."

Molly grabbed Cindy by the arms. "Cindy, stop. You'll get in trouble." She pulled Cindy up from the floor and held her by the arms.

Cindy stopped struggling and stood with Molly. "Better me than you. You can win state, I'm just along for the ride. I don't need a scholarship."

Andrea sat on the dirty floor of the bathroom, blood running from her nose. "Look what you did!" Tears mixed with the blood. "I think you broke my nose."

Blood oozed through Andrea's fingers and dripped onto the front of her gym shirt.

Loud footsteps drew closer and Ms. Andersen, the gym teacher, ran around the corner. Her wide-eyed gaze traveled from Andrea to Cindy.

"What the hell is going on here?"

The other girls spread out behind their teacher whispering to each other.

Molly opened her mouth to answer.

Cindy spoke first. "Andrea jumped on Molly, so I jumped on Andrea." Cindy glared at the teacher. "She was trying to get Molly suspended so she'd miss state."

Ms. Andersen handed Andrea paper towels for her nose. "Is that true, Andrea?"

Andrea's narrowed eyes glittered with tears. "No, Cindy started it. They attacked me." Tears mixed with the blood on Andrea's cheeks.

Molly frowned. "That's not true. You pushed me."

"Did anyone else see what happened?" When nobody spoke up, Ms. Anderson sighed. "Well, I guess the only fair thing to do is send you to the office and let Mr. Roberts deal with this." She

pointed to the door. "Go. You can change after you've finished in

the office."

Cindy pleaded with the teacher. "Ms. A., that ain't right.

Molly didn't do anything. She shouldn't get in trouble."

"Mr. Roberts can argue with you. I have a class to teach."

She turned and called to the other girls. "Let's go, the show's over.

Time for class." The girls followed her out to the gym.

Molly grabbed Cindy's arm. "Come on." She frowned at

Andrea. "Why did you do this? You could have done well at state."

Andrea laughed. "Oh, I'll still get to go. But when Mr.

Roberts hears my story *you* won't get to compete."

Molly's stomach clenched.

Cindy snorted. "Mr. Roberts isn't stupid, Andrea. He'll know

you're lying." She pulled on Molly. "Let's go." They left the locker

room with Andrea trailing behind them, holding her nose with paper

towels from the bathroom.

In the principal's office, again, Molly waited to explain what

happened. Her insides felt like hamburger. What if he didn't believe

her, and she didn't get to go to state?

Mr. Roberts observed her over the rim of his glasses. He sat back in his chair and crossed his arms over his round middle.

"Well, Molly. I can say this is the first time I've had one girl be the catalyst for fights between male and female fighters."

Molly cleared her throat. "I'm sorry, Mr. Roberts."

He nodded. "I assume this had something to do with the other altercation?"

"Sort of." She stared at the desk and rushed through an explanation. "Andrea is mad that I'm dating Hayden, and she wanted to get me suspended for fighting so I'd have to miss state on Saturday. Cindy fought her instead, so I wouldn't get suspended because the college scouts will be there to decide if they want to give me a scholarship which I need because my mother can't afford college and if I get suspended and can't go I don't know how…"

Mr. Roberts held up a hand and closed his eyes. "Molly, I have no intention of suspending you."

She sagged in her chair and tears of relief filled her eyes. "Thank you, Mr. Roberts."

He raised his eyebrows. "But you need to consider this a warning. Any more incidents of this nature and I will take action."

He leaned his elbows on the desktop. "College scouts look for athletes who are able to follow the rules, Molly. They might not want someone with discipline marks on their records."

She swallowed and nodded. "I understand. But, Mr. Roberts, how am I supposed to control what other people do? Andrea started this, and I tried to walk away."

He sighed. "If you figure out the answer to that question, you let me know. I can only say this, stay away from the ones who are causing the trouble and hope for the best. Andrea will serve suspension for a couple days. That should take her out of the equation."

Molly's stomach twisted with guilt. Because of this mess, Andrea wouldn't run at state. At least she was only a junior, she'd have another shot. "What about Cindy? She was only defending me."

Mr. Roberts shook his head. "She's a good friend. But she knew the consequences for fighting. I'm sorry but she will also serve suspension."

Tears spilled over onto Molly's cheeks. Guilt stabbed her again.

Mr. Roberts gave her a sad smile. "The best thing for you to do now is to honor your friend's sacrifice and do the best you can at state."

"But it's my fault. All of it. Hayden and Trevor, Cindy and Andrea, they fought because of me." Molly grabbed a tissue from the desk and wiped her eyes.

Mr. Roberts chucked. "No, they fought because they chose to, not because you made them. Like you said, you can't control what other people do." He folded his hands on the desk. "You can, however, make them understand you don't want them fighting for you. Maybe telling them what you want will help keep this mess from getting any bigger."

Molly nodded. He was right. She needed to tell them what she wanted. And what she wanted was for her friend and boyfriend to stay out of trouble.

Mr. Roberts stood, the leather chair squeaking in protest from his weight. Molly rose, too, facing him across the desk.

"Go back to class, Molly. I need to speak to Andrea and Cindy. And I'll need to call your mother."

"She's at work." Her stomach ached thinking about the disappointment her mom would feel. "Thank you, Mr. Roberts, for believing me."

He inclined his head. "Don't worry, I've heard lots of stories over the years. I know when kids are lying. Good luck at state, Molly. I hope you get what you're working for."

She smiled her thanks and left the office.

CHAPTER TWENTY-FIVE

HAYDEN

Mike sat next to Hayden on the locker-room bench tying his cleats. "Did you hear the news?"

Hayden groaned. "What news?"

Loud talk and slamming metal doors surrounded them while the team got ready for practice. Hayden pulled on his practice jersey and waited for Mike's response.

"Andrea and Cindy had a fight today in gym. They both got suspended."

Hayden stared at Mike. "What? Why were they fighting? Cindy can be a hothead, but she's never violent. Something must have pissed her off."

Mike shrugged. "They were fighting because of your new girlfriend."

Hayden sat on the bench and rubbed his head. "What did Molly have to do with it?" He'd bet his left nut Andrea was to blame.

"Andrea says they jumped her in the bathroom, but nobody believes her. Molly didn't get suspended, just Andrea and Cindy." Mike stood and put his street clothes in his soccer bag. "Cindy kicked her ass. You should see Andrea's face."

Hayden grabbed his bag and followed Mike toward the door. "Did Molly get hurt?"

Mike shook his head. "I don't think so."

They walked out to the field, the chilly fall air carried the smell of dead leaves and mud from the nearby woods where Molly was practicing. Hayden imagined he could smell strawberries, too.

Hayden sighed, wishing practice was over so he could see her. "I'll bet she feels bad. Cindy will miss state now."

"Yeah, I heard she didn't want Molly to get in trouble." Mike dropped a ball to his feet and threw his bag on the bench. "She's a good friend, to take that kind of punishment. And she's cute." He winked at Hayden.

Hayden laughed. "I'll tell her you think so. She's tough though. You sure you want to mess with her?" He jogged away, and Mike passed him the ball. Hayden dribbled toward the box then turned to face Mike.

"Go ahead, tell her. I'm a goalie, guys kick balls at my head. I'm tough too." He pointed to his feet and Hayden passed back, laughing harder. They ran to join the team for warm-ups.

**

After practice, Hayden drove to the lot near the cross-country course to pick up Molly. He saw the team stretching and settled in to wait. He popped in a cassette and sang along with the music.

Leaning his head back on the seat, he closed his eyes, picturing Molly. She was smart and funny, that's why he loved her, but right now he wasn't thinking about her jokes. His racing pulse and quivering stomach weren't from considering her grades either. It was her soft curls, her smooth pale skin, her long tight legs in her uniform and the way they flexed while she pushed through the woods that made it hard to breathe when he was around her.

Something pounded on the passenger window, and Hayden jumped. His eyes flew open, and he grabbed the steering wheel, hitting the horn on accident. The girls walking in front of his car jerked to a stop and glared through the window.

Molly opened the door laughing. "Sorry, I didn't realize you were sleeping." She leaned over and kissed Hayden on the cheek.

He took a deep breath. "What kind of hello is that?" He held her shoulders and kissed her.

She sighed and put her hands on his chest. "You know what?" she whispered between kisses.

"What?" Hayden's whisper shook. He pulled her closer and rubbed his hands along her sides.

"We should make this our official hello. None of that cheeky stuff." Molly giggled and kissed his cheek again.

"Okay, but we might get in trouble doing this in the middle of school."

He kissed her again then let go, his heart thrumming in his chest. She was sweaty and had mud on her legs from the wet trail but looked better than ever. He craved more than a kiss. He started the car to keep himself from doing something stupid, like pulling her into the backseat.

"True, but it's a better reason to get sent to the office than fighting." Molly touched his hand. "I'm sure you've heard. Nothing stays secret for long in this little school."

Hayden caressed her cheek and nodded. "Tell me what happened while I drive. I want to get out of here."

"Can we run by my house, so I can change? I don't want to meet your family looking like I just ran six miles. Which I did." She pointed to her messy ponytail and sweaty clothes.

Hayden nodded, his gaze lingering on her bare legs. "Sure, if you want me to." He backed the car out and they left the lot. While he drove, she recounted the fight and Mr. Roberts' advice.

Molly stared out the window. "I hate that Cindy doesn't get to run at state now."

Hayden shook his head. "It's not fair. It's Andrea's fault, but if Cindy hadn't stepped in, you would be the one missing state."

"Yes, but Mr. Roberts was right. Cindy knew the rules. And she only did it to save my chance." She wiped a tear from her cheek. "I don't want this to happen again. From her or you. No more fighting. Please, I can't stand it, knowing it's because of me." Another tear followed the first.

Hayden pulled into her driveway and cut the engine. He turned to Molly and held her hands. "It's not your fault. I won't go looking for a fight, but I won't let anyone talk about you."

She frowned. "Hayden, promise me you won't fight anymore. I don't care what people say." She glanced at their hands. "I've been thinking."

Hayden groaned. "Not again. Last time that led me to the friend zone."

Molly smiled and shook her head. "Not this time. I've been thinking about what I want for my life. I want to go to school in California, so I need that scholarship from UCLA."

The familiar hollowness spread inside his chest whenever he thought about her going away to school. He wanted to be with her, but he also wanted her to be happy.

"You'll get it. They'd be crazy not to take you." He rubbed her cheek again. "But I don't want you to go away."

"That's the other thing. I want to be with you." She leaned in and kissed him with a feather soft touch of her lips. "I love you."

Hayden gazed into her eyes and smiled. "What did you say?"

Molly grinned. "I said, I love you."

Hayden hugged her. "God, I've been dying to hear you say that. I never thought you'd feel that way."

She giggled. "That's because you're an idiot."

Hayden laughed and squeezed her tighter. "Takes one to know one."

"That's why I love you. Because you're so nice."

Hayden kissed her, his heart pounding to the rhythm of their rapid breaths. A smile stretched across his face. "Get changed so we can go to my house."

Molly leaned back in her seat. "You'd better wait out here. My mom wouldn't want you in the house alone with me. Besides, the way I feel, if you came inside, Andrea would have the last laugh and Cindy would kill me." Molly's cheeks flared red under her molten silver eyes.

Hayden swallowed, heat flooding his body, too. "I think you're right." He reached out and touched her face. "But would that be such a bad thing? I thought we decided we didn't care what anyone else thinks?"

Molly bit her lip, tilting her head.

Hayden held up a hand. "It wasn't a request. I didn't mean I wanted to come in with you."

She raised an eyebrow. "Don't you?" A smile tugged at the corners of her lips.

"Well, that's not what I meant either. I meant…, I do, but I didn't… you shouldn't think that's why I came here or that you had to…" Hayden groaned. His dad was right. Girls were way better at knowing what they needed.

Molly laughed. "I know what you meant." She opened the door and a blast of cold air entered the car. Hayden welcomed the chill. "I'll be back in a few minutes."

Hayden leaned back in the seat again and laid his head on the headrest. "I'll be here, cooling down."

She rolled her eyes then closed the door. Hayden drew a deep breath while Molly ran toward the house. Her ponytail bobbed on her shoulders and her legs flashed in the late afternoon sunlight. The quiver returned to Hayden's stomach. He sucked in another big breath and waited until Molly shut the door to exhale.

"So much for cooling down." Hayden blew out the breath and turned the key. The music came back on and he turned it up until the windows vibrated. Maybe Bon Jovi could help him forget the feel of her body on his.

CHAPTER TWENTY-SIX

MOLLY

Hayden drove through the quiet streets of his neighborhood. The well-manicured lawns and ginormous brick houses were the total opposite of Molly's side of town. Her stomach twisted at the difference between her and Hayden. But when he looked at her and smiled, she forgot they came from two different worlds.

Hayden pulled into his driveway and parked. When the engine quit, Molly glanced at the house. Her hand trembled on the door handle and her bouncing knee shook the car.

"Relax. My parents are dying to meet you." Hayden patted her knee. The heat from his hand seared through the thin fabric of her leggings.

"I'm not good at small talk with strangers. Don't let me make an idiot of myself." Molly placed her hand on Hayden's.

"I thought we were both idiots. Nothing wrong with that is there?" Hayden winked. "But if it makes you feel better, I promise to save you from any idiotic ramblings."

She laughed. "Thanks."

Hayden paused and frowned. He hesitated with his hand on the door.

"What is it?" Molly asked.

"I should warn you. My mom can be overprotective. You're the first girl I've ever brought home to meet them, and I'm sure my mom will be weird about it."

Molly swallowed the lump in her throat. "Will she not like me?"

Hayden rubbed her hair, damp from the quick shower she'd taken. "No, that's not it. She might ask lots of questions." He kissed her and smiled. "Just be yourself and she'll love you like I do."

She sighed and hugged Hayden's neck. "Those leading man lines are getting to me."

Hayden laughed. "Then my plan is working. Come on, let's go inside. I'm starving."

Molly got out of the car. The smell of the grill cut through the cold air, reminding her of summer days and freedom.

Hayden met her on her side and took her hand, leading her to the front door. "After you." He opened the door and waved his arm. She stepped inside.

The huge living room, filled with soft greens and peaches, couldn't ease the tension that threatened to choke Molly. Hayden's mom sat on the end of a beige floral-patterned sofa. The brass lamp on the end table cast a soft glow on her shiny dark hair. She looked up from her book and smiled, her green eyes the same shade as Hayden's.

Hayden's dad entered from the kitchen. Nothing of his light brown hair and blue eyes had been passed down to Hayden. He smiled at Molly and raised his eyebrows. She thought she saw him wink at Hayden.

Hayden held her hand. He squeezed then addressed his parents. "Hey, Mom, Dad." Another squeeze. "This is Molly."

Her throat constricted, and she couldn't breathe. She held on to Hayden's hand like she was drowning, and he was the life jacket. His mom placed her book on the end table and came to them. She held out her hand and Molly took it, her own trembling.

"Welcome. I'm Nancy." Her smile was friendly, but cautious.

Molly returned it with a nervous grin. "It's nice to meet you, Mrs. Bishop."

Hayden's dad s approached them with his hand extended. "It's nice to finally meet you, Molly. We've heard a lot about you."

His smile was warm and reminded her of Hayden. Maybe Hayden did get a piece of his dad. She felt a fraction of the fear ease. "It's nice to meet you both."

Hayden put his arm around her waist and his mom flinched. Molly looked away. "My dad's name is Hayden, too, but everyone calls him James. That's his middle name."

James nodded. "You can use our first names, Molly. We're informal with Hayden's friends."

"Thank you, James." Molly smiled at Hayden. "Since you and your dad share a name, does that mean I can call you Junior?" Hayden wrinkled his nose and shook his head.

His mom chuckled, patting Hayden on the shoulder. "We only call him that when he does something idiotic like his father."

Molly smiled at his dad's wounded groan.

He put an arm around Nancy and kissed her cheek. "I try to be good but sometimes I slip up. That's why I have you dear, to keep me in line."

His parent's teasing lightened the mood and eased Molly's nervousness. She glanced at Hayden. "I didn't realize idiocy was an inherited trait. You come by it honestly I see."

Hayden raised an eyebrow. "My mom say's my dad was worse at my age. The gene weakens with each generation, so my own kids should be good." He winked at his mom.

She laughed. "That's a long way off so we'll have to wait and see. Are you hungry? Your father is making burgers." His mom glanced at Hayden's arm still around Molly's waist.

She wished he would let go. She wanted his mom to like her, and from the concerned look on her face, she didn't like Hayden's casual touches. Hayden must have thought the opposite. He pulled Molly closer and raised an eyebrow, his lips pulling up at one corner.

His dad cleared his throat. "Yes, I should get them on the grill. The fire is ready. Hayden, meet me outside and give me a hand."

His mom patted his dad's hand. "I'll get the salad ready. Molly, would you mind helping me?"

She gulped. "No, I don't mind."

His mom and dad both smiled and walked hand in hand to the kitchen. Once they left, Hayden kissed Molly on the temple. "Sorry but separating us is code for 'my mom wants to talk to you alone'."

Her stomach filled with bricks. "What? Why? Please don't leave me alone with her."

Hayden grinned. "She won't hurt you. She'll ask you questions about me. I told you she's overprotective."

Hayden held Molly by the hips and kissed her softly. He released her, smiling at her sigh. "Just don't mention the conversation we had in the car and you should be fine."

Molly rolled her eyes. "Thanks for the advice."

They walked into the kitchen. White cabinets lined the walls. The dark blue tiled backsplash provided a bold contrast. The butcher-block counter on the island was bigger than her whole kitchen at home.

His mom stood at the white farmhouse sink washing lettuce in a spinner. She glanced over her shoulder and smiled. "Could you give me a hand and chop those carrots and peppers for the salad?"

"Sure, Nancy."

Hayden squeezed her waist and winked. "I better go help my dad." He grabbed the tongs and left through the French doors leading to the back yard.

Molly's pulse raced as Hayden walked away. She grabbed the knife by the cutting board and chopped the carrots. The task was familiar but her shaking hands made it more difficult.

Nancy placed the salad bowl on the island next to Molly. "So, Molly, Hayden told us you're running in the state cross-country meet this weekend."

Glad for the safe topic, Molly relaxed. "Yes, we run on Saturday. I'm nervous but excited, too."

Nancy nodded and picked up the vegetables Molly had chopped so far. She tossed them in the salad bowl. Molly continued to chop trying not to cut off her finger with the sharp knife.

"He also said you're trying to get a scholarship." Nancy chuckled. "He likes to talk about you. How long have you known him?"

Molly swallowed to loosen her throat. "We met last year during track."

"I remember him mentioning that." She scooped up more cut vegetables and placed them in the bowl. "Then you dated Trevor."

Molly's hand slipped, and a piece of carrot popped across the island and fell to the floor. Nancy picked it up and threw it in the sink.

"Yes, I did." She drew a shaky breath. Where was Nancy going with this?

"Trevor and Hayden have been friends for a long time. So have James and Trevor's father, Stan." She sighed. "Molly, I have to be honest with you."

Molly stopped chopping and met Nancy's concerned gaze. "Honesty is good. It makes things easier to understand." Would Hayden's mom would kick her out before or after dinner?

Nancy frowned and squeezed her lips together. "I don't want you to take this the wrong way, but I need to know why you're with my son when you were dating his best friend."

Molly glanced toward the back door where Hayden laughed with his dad. His eyes turned to her and he waved through the window. She tried to draw strength from his smile.

"Trevor was wrong for me. He lied and made me feel like I was to blame for every problem we had. Hayden was the one to help me see I deserved better. And he was right. He makes me feel special, and I want to do the same for him." She smiled at Nancy. "I'm with him because he wants to be with me, too."

Nancy stared at her for a moment, lips pursed. "I understand what you mean about Trevor. He and Hayden have always been competitive. They've fought over many things through the years. But never a girl. I don't want this to be another battle between them." Her green eyes were serious. "I want to be sure you aren't doing this to start fights."

Molly's eyes prickled. "I wouldn't do that. I don't want him to fight anybody, especially not Trevor." God, this was worse than she expected.

Nancy's nose whistled with her deep breath. "I hope not. He's already been in two fights, that's more than enough." She grabbed the rest of the veggies and put them in the bowl, carrying it to the table in the next room.

Molly blinked back her tears and glanced out the door. Hayden watched her with a frown. He said something to his dad, then came back inside.

"What's wrong?" He glanced at the door where his mom had disappeared.

Molly shook her head and tried to smile. "Nothing. Everything's fine." She blinked fast to clear her eyes.

"You're a terrible liar." He rubbed her cheek. "Did my mom upset you?"

"No, it's fine. She and I were just talking." She didn't want to start trouble between Hayden and his mom.

"She upset you. Just forget it." He leaned his forehead on hers. "It doesn't matter what she thinks." Hayden squeezed her trembling hands.

"It matters, Hayden. I want her to know I'm not just using you to get back with Trevor." Molly raised their hands to her cheek. "I love you, and your family should know that."

"Ahem."

They both jumped.

"Hayden did Dad need anything else?" His mom stood with her hands on her hips, watching them from the doorway. She glanced at Molly with a small smile.

Hayden stood and faced his mom. He lifted his chin and placed a hand on Molly's shoulder. "Nope, he said he's almost finished. I thought I might help more in here." He glared at his mom and Molly's stomach ached.

Nancy raised an eyebrow. "Well, you two can set the table. She did an excellent job chopping carrots during my interrogation." Nancy winked at her. "Which she passed."

Hayden rolled his eyes. "Mom be nice. She's nervous enough." He squeezed her shoulder. "My mom thinks you'll steal away her little boy. She forgets I'm almost eighteen, not eight."

"Someday you'll understand, Hayden. No matter how old you are, you'll always be my little boy. Sorry if I can be overbearing." She handed him a stack of plates. "Now be a good little boy and set these on the table."

"Yes, Mommy. Come on Molly, I'll rescue you."

Molly grinned at their banter, but she still had the weight of fear in her gut. She followed Hayden to the dining room and helped set the table for dinner.

"Sorry my mom's being weird." Hayden laid the last fork on the table then hugged her.

"It's okay."

Hayden pulled out a chair. "You can sit here by me. I'll protect you." He smiled. "And I can hold your hand under the table."

"Right, because that will make your mom like me more." Molly slapped his shoulder. "Your idiot gene is kicking in."

"Maybe, but you heard my dad. Sometimes it's uncontrollable." Hayden glanced toward the kitchen then kissed her.

Her stomach quivered again, but this time she enjoyed it. "I hope your mom didn't see that," she whispered.

Hayden tucked her hair behind her ear. His fingers tickled her neck and Molly sighed.

The doors to the patio snapped shut, and they jumped apart. Hayden's dad came in the dining room carrying a plate of burgers.

"I hope you're both hungry." He winked at Molly. "I know how Hayden can eat. I hope you're not one of those girls who thinks eating is overrated."

Molly smiled and shook her head. "No. I run six to eight miles a day. I like to eat."

He laughed. "Ahh, that's the spirit." He set the plate on the table and took his seat. "I think we'll get along just fine, Molly, because I like to eat, too. But I only run if someone's chasing me."

She snickered, and Hayden smiled.

Nancy came in from the kitchen. She set ketchup and mustard on the table. "Dig in everyone." She sat next to James and patted his hand. "The burgers look great. You even toasted the buns, nice touch." She grabbed a burger off the plate and added the condiments.

"Yeah, Dad, thanks." Hayden handed a burger to Molly then put one on his plate.

"Thanks." She dished salad into their bowls. Molly looked up and caught his parent's exchanging a glance. She quickly looked down and took a bite of her burger.

After a moment, Nancy spoke. "Hayden, I forgot to tell you. You got mail today."

Hayden stopped his fork midway to his mouth. "What was it?"

Nancy smiled. "Your acceptance letter for Purdue."

Molly's bite of burger turned to dust in her mouth. Purdue? She glanced at Hayden.

He frowned at his mom. "That's great." He stuck a bite of salad in his mouth.

"Nancy, you know he doesn't want to go there." James smirked at Nancy's glare. "He only applied to make you happy."

"That's not true. Purdue is a great school. And I'm not just saying that because it's my alma mater." Nancy took a bite of burger and looked at Hayden.

Molly sipped her water to unstick the burger. "I didn't know you had applied there." Indiana wasn't even on her list of maybes. What if Hayden ended up there? She'd never get to see him.

"I applied to lots of places." He winked at her. "But I haven't heard from my first choices yet."

"Where do you want to go, Molly?" James asked.

"Well, my first choice is UCLA. The scout will be at state this weekend. If I do well enough, they should offer me assistance."

Nancy smiled. The long distance from Purdue probably sounded perfect to her.

"That's ambitious. What do you intend to study?"

"I haven't decided yet. Either business with an emphasis in biology or maybe psychobiology." She bit into her burger while Hayden's parents stared at her.

James spoke first. "I don't think I even know what psychobiology is."

Hayden laughed and leaned over to kiss Molly on the head. "I guess I forgot to mention she isn't just beautiful, and a good runner, she's the smartest one in our class."

Molly's cheeks prickled with heat. "Hayden's making that up. I'm not the smartest." She smiled at James. "Psychobiology is the study of the biological basis for behavior and mental phenomena." She grinned. "Maybe I can isolate the gene for the idiocy trait in males and become famous."

Nancy laughed. "Molly, if you could do that, women around the world would worship you." She smiled at Hayden and his dad while they shook their heads.

Hayden touched Molly's hand. "I can major in management, so I can help her take care of her genetics business. I'm sure the world will want her to fix us damaged men."

A swooping feeling filled her chest at the vision he painted for their future together. She touched his arm. "What should I call the business?"

Hayden thought for a moment. "How about Molly's Man Menders. Maybe you could develop a vaccine or something." He held her hand in his. "I'll be a guinea pig for you. Then you won't have to put up with my idiotness."

"I told you, it's cute when you act silly."

James laughed, and Molly jumped. She had forgotten his parents were there watching them. She took a bite of salad, ignoring the fire on her face.

"See, Nancy. No worries. Hayden found someone who knows how to handle him. And you thought he'd be living with us forever."

Nancy smirked. "Well, let's not rush things. I'm in no hurry for him to grow up."

Hayden groaned. "Enough with the kid stuff, Mom."

His dad laughed. "Don't bother. You'll always be baby to her."

"Pink Floyd. "Molly pointed with her fork. "My mom's favorite band."

"Smart, athletic, likes to eat, knows her music," his dad said as he shook his head. "Hayden, you'll have to work hard to keep up with her."

"Nope," he said, nudging Molly with his arm. "She'll wait for me. I'm silly and cute."

His mom laughed and Molly felt her shoulders finally relax as they finished eating.

"Well, it's time to study." Hayden stood and grabbed his plate.

Molly glanced at Hayden's mom. "Do you mind?"

Nancy raised her eyebrows. "Well,"

"Go ahead. I'll help clean up the table." His dad gestured to the dishes.

Nancy closed her mouth, shaking her head at James. "You get to load the dishwasher."

She smiled at Hayden's parents. "Thank you for dinner, it was great. Hayden wasn't lying about your barbecue skills."

James beamed at her. "I do love to grill. Come over anytime."

Hayden took Molly's plate from her hands. "We'll be in the rec room downstairs."

Molly followed him to the kitchen where he rinsed their plates and put them in the dishwasher.

Hayden grabbed her hand and pulled. "Come on, let's get out of here before my mom changes her mind and finds laundry for us to do or something."

After retrieving their backpacks from his car, Hayden led her downstairs. Molly sighed with relief, eager to be alone and away from his Nancy's overprotective eyes.

CHAPTER TWENTY-SEVEN

HAYDEN

Hayden looked around at the brown paneled walls of his basement rec room. Years of good memories hung in the pictures on the walls; Christmases, birthday parties, hanging out with friends. But nothing matched the excitement he felt sitting with Molly on the overstuffed chocolate-colored leather sofa.

She read her history book. Hayden leaned back against the arm of the couch facing her and pretended to study statistics. But every few sentences he found his gaze drifting to her.

Molly smiled, keeping her eyes on her book. "If you don't actually look at your book, I don't think you'll learn anything."

Hayden grinned and put his book on the coffee table. He snatched Molly's from her hands.

"Hey, give that back." She reached for the book.

He held it above his head. "How bad do you want it?"

Molly tickled his armpit and he laughed. She giggled and grabbed the book when he dropped his arm to avoid her fingers.

He grabbed her wrist, pulling her toward him. "Cheater. I wanted you to offer me something."

She put her hands on his chest. "Sorry, what did you want?"

Hayden shrugged. "Hmm. What do you want to offer?"

Molly pressed her chest against his. He put his arms around her and tried to swallow. The fresh scent of her hair and skin surrounded him, and he imagined the taste.

"I can think of a few things." She wiggled her eyebrows. "They might be worth something to you."

He tried not to pant like a puppy. "Like?"

She moved her hands to his neck. "Like this."

Her kiss made Hayden forget his effort. He breathed like a dog on a hot sidewalk in the middle of July.

He touched her, kissed her, unable to stop. She leaned even closer, her whole body lying on top of his. He rubbed her back, her sides, and, before he could think not to, he touched the softness of her breasts.

Molly gasped but didn't pull away. She pressed her hips closer, circling against him, sending his heartrate through the roof.

Hayden reached under her shirt, caressing the skin of her back. The quiet moans echoing in her chest sparked a need in him that was almost impossible to contain.

But he'd promised to treat her better, so he pulled his hands away. "I'm sorry." He wanted her, but he had to respect her. She deserved it.

"Why?" Her breath raced, her eyes the color of liquid steel. She kissed him again.

Hayden moved his hands back to her face and held her. "I don't want to be like Trevor. I want this someday, but I want it to be special. And at the right time."

She wrinkled her nose. "Are you sure you're not actually eighty?"

Hayden laughed. "I didn't know respect was so out-of-date."

Molly still lay on top of him. Her quick breaths fanned his face. "I know you love me, but this has nothing to do with Trevor. When is the right time? Because this sure feels like it."

Hayden smiled. "Well for starters, not when my mom and dad could walk in." He pressed a kiss on her lips.

Molly took a deep breath and pushed herself off his chest. Sitting, she pulled Hayden's hands to hers.

"I guess you're right. Your mom would freak out." She ran her fingers through her hair. "All our friends talk about is who's had sex. That's what caused our problems. Maybe we *shouldn't* think about it yet."

Hayden grinned. "Molly, I don't think of having sex with you."

She raised her eyebrows. "Oh? Then what do you think about while we're kissing?"

"I want to make love, not just have sex."

Tears filled Molly's eyes and she smiled. "If Cindy heard that she would faint." She hugged him.

Hayden buried his face in her long blond hair and slid his hands to her waist. "Maybe we should study in case my mom comes downstairs." Unless he could get his parents to leave for a while.

"Okay, but I think you should sit over there to reduce the temptation for me." She pointed to an armchair.

Hayden laughed and picked up his stats book. "Fine, but that only makes it easier for me to stare at you."

He hopped into the chair and threw his legs over the arm. Molly laughed and opened her history book.

After a few minutes, loud footsteps echoed on the stairs. Hayden's parents arrived carrying bowls of ice cream. They stopped at the bottom of the steps and eyed them with wide eyes.

"See, I told you they would be studying." His dad elbowed his mom in the side. "And you thought they would be watching TV."

She laughed and handed a bowl of ice cream to Molly.

"Chocolate is my favorite. Thanks." Molly dipped her spoon and took a bite.

Hayden accepted the bowl from his dad. "Thanks, Dad."

Instead of leaving, his parents joined Molly on the couch with their bowls. Nancy sat nearest to her. Hayden caught his mom's eye and raised an eyebrow.

His mom smiled. "Is the team ready for the big game tomorrow, Hayden?"

"It'll be a tough game without our best forward." Hayden stabbed his spoon into his ice cream, imagining it was Trevor's face instead of chocolate chunk.

His dad frowned. "I spoke with Stan today. Tim's hearing is set for tomorrow."

Hayden squinted at the mention of Trevor's dad. *That jerk probably paid off the judge to give Tim the worst possible sentence.*

Molly frowned, stirring the ice cream in her bowl. "What will happen to him?"

"The judge overseeing his case is a decent man. He believes in second chances, so he should be lenient. Tim will, more than likely, get credit for the time he served and have to take anger management classes." He smiled at her. "That's maybe not a bad thing for him. He's a hothead on the field."

Hayden laughed. "Yes, but he's also our leading goal scorer. It's a trade-off." He finished his ice cream and sat the bowl on the table.

His mom sighed. "Well, I hope you learn from his mistake, Hayden. Fighting is never the answer to a problem."

Molly stiffened, and Hayden frowned. He narrowed his eyes at his mom. "Sometimes you can't avoid it, Mom, when you have something worth fighting for." He looked at Molly.

She met his eyes and shook her head. "Hayden, your mom is right. I don't want you fighting either."

He grinned at his mom's glare and Molly's worried gaze. "There're no future bouts scheduled so you can both relax."

His dad laughed and patted his mom's knee. "Don't worry, Hayden's boxing days are over. He got what he wanted, right Hayden?"

Sometimes his parents could be such a pain. For crying out loud, his dad acted like Molly wasn't sitting right there.

"Dad, you make it sound like I got a new bike or something." He looked at Molly, his pulse spiked at the memory of their kiss. "She's letting me be with her, but I don't own her." He smiled when she rolled her eyes.

Molly giggled. "Hayden's rehearsing for the part of Romeo in the next play. He's been working on the romantic lines."

His mom's laughter joined hers. "When he was little, his action figures used the lines on the damsel in distress. Superman had the best ones."

Molly's laugh tinkled through the room. Hayden groaned and covered his eyes with his fingers. "Mom, please." He looked at his dad and raised his hands.

"I know better than to get in the middle of this." His dad stood and grabbed the empty ice cream bowls. "I think I'll escape upstairs. Good luck." He smiled at Hayden's helpless smirk.

"Thanks, Dad." Hayden's embarrassment eased when he looked at Molly's smiling face. If it made her look at him that way, he'd take any abuse his mom could dish out.

"Do you have any other stories, Nancy?" Molly winked at Hayden.

His mom stood and walked to the bookshelf. She grabbed a thick book Hayden knew well. He groaned. "Oh, God, Mom, please no. She doesn't want to see those."

She rejoined an eager Molly on the couch and placed the opened book on her lap.

Molly's eyes grew wide and she flushed. "Pictures?" She scooted closer to his mom.

When Molly turned her excited gaze on him, Hayden sighed. He squeezed himself next to her on the cushion. He put an arm around her shoulders and kissed her cheek. "All right, but you have to promise not to laugh."

She giggled. "No promises."

He used his free hand to hold hers.

His mom smiled, gazing at them cuddled together. Hayden met her eyes and she nodded. "Let's get started, shall we?" She and Molly exchanged a smile.

While his mom flipped through the pages of his childhood, Molly awed and giggled. His mom laughed along with her, and Hayden relaxed. Molly had won her over. If there was one thing his mom respected, it was anyone who loved her son like she did.

***

Later that night, after he took Molly home, Hayden lay awake in his bed thinking about her. He pictured her smiling face while his mom told story after story of him as a kid.

How was it possible to fall harder for Molly? He already loved her and wanting her was a given. But seeing her interact with his mom today made him realize he didn't just want to date Molly now. He wanted to be with her forever.

Hayden sighed and rubbed his face. He was only seventeen, too young to be thinking of forever. Right?

After a knock on his door, he sat and rubbed a hand through his hair. "Come in."

His mom peeked around the door. "Got a minute?"

Great, she'd come with a lecture of all the reasons he should take it slow with Molly. "Sure."

She came in and sat at the foot of his bed. "I wanted to talk to you… about Molly." She twisted her hands together.

"What about?" Hayden tried to keep a defensive tone out of his words.

His mom looked at her hands and sighed. "I'm sorry I upset her today. I didn't mean to."

Hayden frowned. "She's the one you need to apologize to for that."

"Yes, but I also needed to apologize to you. I can tell she means a lot to you. When I upset her, it affects you, too." She put her hand on his ankle. "She's a very nice girl, I like her."

BREAKING THE BRO CODE

Hayden grinned. "I know, so do I."

His mom laughed. "It's obvious there's more to your feelings than just liking her." She squeezed his ankle and let go.

Hayden was glad his room was dark, so his mom couldn't see his face turn red. "You're right. I love her, Mom."

His mom covered her lips with her fingers and nodded. She blinked so fast she looked like a cartoon.

Hayden whispered, "Mom, when did you know you wanted to be with dad forever?"

She wiped her eye and sighed. "It took a while. Your father was a bit of a loose cannon in the early days. He liked to joke and goof around. He flirted with me, but he flirted with everyone. I didn't know he was serious about me until he asked me out. We dated for a year and he started talking about getting married. I thought he was still joking, but then he knelt down and gave me a ring." She smiled.

Hayden frowned. "How old were you?"

"We were twenty-one. We'd just graduated college." She gave Hayden a curious look. "Why are you asking me about this?"

Hayden shrugged and avoided her gaze. "I can't imagine being with anyone else but her. But I don't know if I should feel that way. I'm only seventeen." He leaned his head on the headboard and closed his eyes. "She's all I can think about though."

His mom's soft laugh floated around the quiet room. Hayden opened his eyes and looked at her. He didn't feel like laughing.

"What you feel, is how every teenager feels the first time they fall in love."

He shook his head. "But how do you know when it's forever?"

"You'll know. But I agree, seventeen is too young to think that way. You need to give your relationship time to bloom. If Molly is the one, she'll still be there. That's when you'll know."

Hayden nodded, but he didn't completely believe his mom. She might be underestimating his feelings.

"Can I ask you something now?"

"Sure."

She cleared her throat, glancing at her hands.

Hayden had second thoughts about his easy yes.

"I noticed you're very comfortable... uhm touching her. I know times are different, but I want to know for sure you and she are being... careful."

"Careful with?" Hayden's eyes grew wide. Oh, God, she was talking about sex. He and his mom talked about a lot of things, but he couldn't believe she brought up this subject. Shouldn't his dad be in here instead? "Mom, please. I don't want to talk about this with you."

She stared at the ceiling and took a deep breath. "Well, it's my responsibility and I need to know."

Hayden covered his head with a pillow. He remembered his dad's advice, better just to answer the question and end the torture. "Molly and I haven't... you know."

"Maybe you haven't yet, but you might want to, and I want to know you understand the possible consequences."

Hayden fought the urge to run from the room. If Molly found out about this she would die laughing.

"I know what sex is, Mom, and what it causes. Don't worry, we aren't doing it, but if we were, I know what to do." He pressed the pillow down on his burning face. "I mean I know what to do to prevent..." He groaned. "I mean I know about condoms, okay?" He lifted the pillow and glared at his mom.

His mom laughed. "I'm sorry I embarrassed you. Your father said he wouldn't talk about this with you because he was sure you already knew. But I thought one of us should."

"Dad was right, Mom. You probably could have avoided this torture."

She pushed herself off the bed. "Well, I feel better knowing we talked about it." She walked to the door and turned back around. "By the way, I think you made a good choice. Molly is a sweet girl. She seems like she has a good head on her shoulders."

"She does, Mom, and thanks." He grinned. "But I won't tell her about this conversation. She'd never let me live it down. Thanks to you, she already thinks I'm a mama's boy."

His mom chuckled. "Well, there's nothing wrong with that. Good night, Hayden."

"Good night."

When she closed the door, Hayden sighed with relief. He scooted down under the covers and lay back on the pillow. He replayed their conversation in his head.

His mom was right. He'd know when it was forever. Molly's face again filled his mind and he smiled. Forever had already begun.

CHAPTER TWENTY-EIGHT

MOLLY

The alarm beeped and *That's What Friends Are For...* blared from the speaker. Molly reached over and slapped the off button. She buried her head under the pillow.

"Molly let's go. You'll be late." Her mom knocked on her door. "I turned the shower on for you."

She groaned and jumped out of bed. Grabbing her clothes, she ran to the bathroom. The hot water was flowing, and she didn't want to miss it. Hayden invaded her mind as soon as she stood under the warm water. Her lips tingled thinking about their kisses.

She grinned and rushed through her shower routine. The water cooled so Molly hurried, and then turned off the water and toweled herself dry. The shrill ringing of the phone echoed from the kitchen.

"I got it!" She ran to the kitchen and grabbed the receiver from the wall. "Hello?"

"Hey, girl." Cindy's voice greeted Molly. "So, did you meet his parents? What were they like? Did they like you or are you guys going to have a secret romance?" Molly smiled, used to Cindy's unfiltered enthusiasm.

"Yes, they were cool. His mom took a while to warm up, but after bonding over Hayden's baby book, she was nicer."

Cindy chortled. "I'll bet Hayden loved that. Was he embarrassed?"

Molly grinned. "You know Hayden. He laughed it off. I think he was just happy his mom talked to me."

"So, is he a mama's boy or what?"

"Totally." Molly giggled. "I think he tells her everything. Kind of like me and my mom." She wrapped the phone cord around her fingers. "It's nice, though. It shows he has a sensitive side."

Cindy's snort hurt Molly's ear. "We knew that, Molly. He's an old man in a teenage body. A hot body for sure."

"So, what are you going to do today while the rest of us have to go to school?"

"Oh, my mom has plans for me. She's making me write a paper describing the detrimental effects of fighting." Cindy huffed into the phone. "It's bogus. I don't know why she can't just let me enjoy my time off."

Guilt squirmed in Molly's stomach. "I'm sorry, Cindy. This is my fault."

"It's not your fault, it's Andrea's. She started it."

Molly smirked. "But it was me she started it with. You didn't need to step in and get yourself in trouble."

"No biggie. Like I said, you need to be at state. That's your shot. Win and get that scholarship to UCLA."

Molly sighed at the mention of school. She told Cindy about Hayden's acceptance to Purdue. "What if he goes there and I'm in California? We won't ever get to see each other."

"Molly." Cindy's voice took on the motherly tone she used when she thought Molly was being stupid. "You can't let that affect what you do. You need to do what's best for you."

"I know. But, God, I'd miss him so much. And what if he found someone else?" She felt a surge of anger for this hypothetical woman.

"If he did, then he wouldn't be worth missing. Focus on winning. Everything else will come when it comes."

"You're right. I need to get through this race. Besides, maybe Hayden will be at the same school." They hadn't talked about it, but she wondered if he had thought the same thing she did. She took a breath. "Are you grounded, or do you think your mom will let you do something tonight?"

Cindy sighed. "She said I'm grounded until I'm dead, but maybe I can write this stupid paper and she'll let me go out. What's up?"

"I want to go watch the soccer game against Altgeld. Everyone is going."

"And you want to watch Hayden lead his team to victory, so you can kiss him when he wins."

Molly laughed. "Yep, you got it. But I'll kiss him either way."

"Don't you go getting easy. Make him work for those kisses. You know what they say about free milk and a cow."

"Are you calling me a cow?"

"Only if you give away your milk." Cindy giggled. "I gotta go. I want to start that paper. I'll convince my mom to let me go to the game. Call me after school, and get my homework for me, too."

Molly sighed. "I'll even do it for you. I owe you big-time."

"Just win at state and get that scholarship, that's how you can pay me back."

"I'll do my best." She smiled, picturing the look on Cindy's face if she won state.

"Later, girl." Cindy clicked off and Molly hung up the phone.

Her mom walked into the kitchen wearing her factory clothes. At least at the factory they could wear jeans. She smiled, her mom made even her old frayed jeans and button-down navy-blue shirt look good.

"Was that Cindy?" She smiled, the corners of her eyes crinkling.

"Yes, she wanted me to get her homework." She sighed. "I'm tired of delivering stuff to people who get suspended because they fought for me."

"Did you tell them to lay off the violence like Mr. Roberts suggested?" Her mom poured a cup of coffee, then stirred in sugar and cream.

"Yes, but they both said the same thing. They would do what they needed to." Molly heaved a loud sigh and sat at the table. "The

BREAKING THE BRO CODE

only one I haven't talked to is Trevor. And I don't want to talk to him."

Her mom held the coffee with both hands. "That's up to you, Molly. But it might help to let him know you've moved on."

Molly groaned and laid her head on the table. "I know. But I don't think it will matter. Trevor will cause trouble until he decides he's finished." She raised her head to look at her mom. "And he doesn't want me back. He just wants to hurt Hayden. And me."

Her mom frowned and sipped her coffee. "Maybe you should ignore him then and not rock the boat."

"I think you're right, Mom. I'll let sleeping dogs lie. And he is a dog."

"Good idea." Her mom checked her watch. "I have to go. I'll be at work until midnight. I picked up an extra shift to be off tomorrow for the race." She put her cup in the sink and hugged Molly. "Have a good day and try to relax."

"Thanks, Mom. I'm planning on going to Hayden's soccer game tonight, but I'll be home early so I can get a good night's sleep."

"Okay. Tell Hayden I said good luck." She smiled then grabbed her purse. Molly closed the door behind her when she left.

Molly sat on the couch with her book bag, bouncing her leg and waiting for Hayden to come get her for school. A happy glow filled her chest. Everything was falling into place, and all she had to do was be there to watch it happen.

***

School passed by in a blur. Trevor wasn't there, and with Andrea suspended, the key drama makers were absent. Molly wished Cindy could have been there to enjoy the day with her.

"Molly are you listening?" Hayden tapped on her forehead with a finger. "Hello?" He leaned his back against the lockers, pulling up his lips in a lopsided grin.

Molly shook her head and smiled. "Sorry, I was thinking about what a great day it's been." She wrapped her arms around his waist and laid her head on his chest. The silky white fabric of his soccer jersey slid against her cheek.

"For a minute, I thought you were planning a way to escape from going to the game tonight." Hayden squeezed her.

"Are you kidding? I wouldn't miss it." She lifted her face and he kissed her.

"Phew, glad I don't have to worry then." He kissed her again, longer this time, and Molly tightened her hold.

"Get a room."

Hayden ended the kiss but didn't let go.

Mike stood next to them with a grin on his face. "You guys are going to get busted."

Hayden laughed. "Why don't you block the view, so nobody sees us?"

Molly slapped Hayden's arm. "Stop it. Besides, he's right. I don't think either of our moms would like to get that phone call from Mr. Roberts. He and my mom are already on a first name basis."

Mike chuckled. "Then you're both welcome. I saved your asses." He nodded his head toward Mr. Roberts walking toward them with another teacher.

Molly and Hayden slid apart and smiled. Mr. Roberts smiled back and stopped in front of them. "Hello, Molly, gentlemen. Good luck with your sports this weekend."

Molly smiled. "Thanks, Mr. Roberts. I know I'm ready."

He looked over his glasses. "Good, good. Did you work on what we talked about yesterday?" He glanced at Hayden for a moment.

"Yes, sir. I took care of it." She shifted her weight to the opposite leg. "What I could, anyway."

"That's all you can do." He winked at Hayden and Mike. "Go get them tonight boys. We haven't beaten Altgeld Academy since I took over here. It'd be nice to get the W."

Hayden said, "We'll do our best. We want that win, too."

Mr. Roberts shook their hands. "I have faith in you. Good luck." He walked away, continuing his conversation with the teacher.

Molly laughed. "Thanks, Mike. We owe you one."

Mike raised his eyebrows. "Well, Hayden knows what I want. He can pay me back. See ya." He patted Molly's shoulder and left.

Molly squinted at Hayden. "What was that about?"

He chuckled and pulled Molly's hips to his. "Mike wants me to tell Cindy he's impressed with her loyalty to you. And that she's cute."

She laughed and rubbed Hayden's arms. His muscles quivered sending shock waves into her stomach. "Does Mike know Cindy isn't allowed to date until she's fifty?"

"Don't think that bothers him." Hayden looked at the floor. "Speaking of moms, I had a funny conversation with mine last night."

Molly stopped rubbing his arms and rested her hands on his chest instead. "What did she say?"

"She wanted to know if you and I were... being careful." He wiggled his eyebrows.

She held back her laugh. "Oh, my God. What did you say?" He made a joke out of this, but it probably had embarrassed him.

"It was torture. Cruel and unusual punishment. I had to say the words sex and condom to my own mother."

Molly's laugh rang through the hallway. "You're such a mama's boy. Any questions about the birds and bees?" He blushed, and she giggled harder.

"Thanks, I knew you'd handle this maturely." He leaned and tickled her neck with his chin. Molly laughed and tried to pull away. "I know how everything works, thanks."

"That's good. I thought maybe I'd have to explain it to you." She slid her hands to his chest.

"Someday. Until then, we'd better go. I have to be at the field in an hour."

Molly grabbed her books and the folder with Cindy's homework. "Let's go. I want to be there when you tell Cindy about Mike."

Hayden's eyes widened. "Aren't you going to tell her? Isn't that girl talk... stuff?" He held her hand while they walked to the door.

Molly glanced up. "Well, you're so good at girl talk with your mom I thought you'd want to tell Cindy." Hayden tickled her sides and she laughed.

He put an arm around her waist. "You're mean. Maybe I shouldn't have told you."

"I'm just teasing. I'll tell Cindy after you leave. She may have colorful things to say and I don't want it to get back to Mike."

Hayden snorted. "I'm sure she will."

In his car, Molly patted Hayden on the arm. "I think it's sweet you and your mom are so close. I was just teasing you about the girl talk stuff."

Hayden touched her cheek, his fingers leaving a trail of heat. "Thanks. And I knew you were teasing." He kissed her for a moment, then started the car. He cranked up the heater against the chill. "But I wouldn't mind some private lessons sometime."

Molly rolled her eyes. "Idiot. You had your chance and you turned me down. Now you have to wait."

"But you're worth it." He winked, and Molly groaned. "Too corny?"

"Only a little. But you know I love it."

"Let's go. Cindy needs her homework and news delivery." He pulled out of the lot and Molly smiled.

Yep, things were falling right into place.

CHAPTER TWENTY-NINE

HAYDEN

Later that night, Hayden sat in the tomb-like locker room with his team at half time. Guys slumped against the lockers or held their heads in their hands. He shared their pain. His muscles ached from the physical play. He'd been beat up on the field, and the refs weren't calling many fouls.

The coach's weak speech did nothing to rouse the team's spirits. Tied 1-1 at halftime against a tough team should be a cause for celebration. Instead, everyone looked like their favorite dog got smashed by the garbage truck.

They'd played like crap and barely scraped by with the one goal which came on a penalty kick when Altgeld's giant center back took Hayden down inside the box. Without Tim, Hayden's normal position in the midfield went to a junior named John, and Hayden had to take up the slack of Tim's forward spot.

So far John had sucked, letting in the opposing goal by missing his man. He'd been unable to chase him down and stop him from scoring. He sat away from the rest of the team on the receiving end of frustrated, angry glances.

Mike sat next to Hayden. He punched Hayden on the arm. "Come on, Captain, give us your words of wisdom."

Hayden frowned at his team. You'd think they were losing by ten the way everyone pouted. Hayden stood and addressed them. "Come on, guys. The game's not over. There's another half to play and we're not losing yet."

The team shook their heads.

Hayden frowned. "Yes, we've played like crap. The refs wouldn't know a foul from their own asshole. The other team is twice our size, and their back line should be the starting defensive line for the Chicago Bears."

Mike snorted. "This is the worst motivational speech I've ever heard."

Some of the guys laughed and Hayden smiled. "My point is, despite this shit, we're tied with a team that has kicked our asses every year for the last twenty years. That tells me we have something the teams of the past didn't have." Faces raised to him.

"What?" John spoke from where he sat behind the team.

Hayden met their eyes one by one, then said the word burning in his heart. "Desire."

A few guys straightened their backs, a couple nodded. Most just looked at Hayden.

Hayden frowned. "We want this win. I know everyone in here wants it. Bad. Bad enough to get it. But we won't get it if we quit. When I look back on this day, I want to say I gave it my all. Not just for me, but for my team, for you, because we're in this together."

Nobody spoke. Nobody moved. Hayden met their eyes again. This time nobody looked away. He saw the fire burning in each one. Except John, who still hung his head.

Hayden jumped on the bench to look down on the others. "What is it you want? Do you want to look back and say you gave up? That you quit on your team because it got too hard?" He looked at the top of John's head. "Do you want to blame someone else for a loss when you quit trying?" The guys answered with loud "Hell no's".

John raised his head and met Hayden's gaze.

Hayden smiled. He yelled above the noise made by his fired-up teammates. "Win or lose we're a team. We play as a team. We lose as a team. But I want to win as a team. Who wants to win with me?"

The guys yelled their approval and slapped each other on the back. Hayden jumped from the bench and joined them. They high fived each other and bumped chests. Mike pulled John into the mix, and the others included him in the fray.

Hayden put his fingers in his mouth and whistled. The noise cut off, and they looked to their captain. Hayden grinned. "Now that you guys are awake, let me tell you how we'll win."

CHAPTER THIRTY

MOLLY

Molly and Cindy sat in the bleachers with the rest of their classmates who came to watch the game. Even with a tied game, Hayden's team had looked dejected when they left the field. She'd caught Hayden's eye, and he smiled at her, but he ran into the locker room with a frown.

When the team came out of the locker room after halftime, the students stood and cheered. She searched for Hayden, smiling when he looked up in the stands to find her, too.

Cindy snorted. "They look better. I wonder what drugs they took in the locker room."

Molly laughed. "Maybe they needed the break. I'm sure someone fired them up." Was it Hayden since he was the captain? They lined up on the field to start the second half.

Cindy bobbed her head. "I'm glad to see they aren't just gonna quit. We don't want quitters at this school." She cupped her hands around her mouth. "Let's go Tigers! Show 'em what you're made of! Knock their asses on the ground and blast it in!"

The students cheered with her. Mr. Roberts turned from his position by the fence to look at Cindy. He shook his head, a small smile on his lips.

Molly laughed. "You're going to get kicked out."

Cindy rolled her eyes. "What are they going to do, suspend me?" She gazed at Mike in the goal. He looked up at Cindy and smiled.

Cindy raised her eyebrows and looked away.

Molly elbowed Cindy in the side. "What's wrong? Don't you want to talk to him?"

"Girl, you don't understand how it works. If I let him know I'm interested right away, he gets bored. You got to let them chase you. Then when you give them attention, they think they've won." She snapped her fingers. "And you got 'em right where they need to be, under your thumb."

Molly shook her head. "You're crazy. Just talk to him. He already thinks you're cute and smart. You shouldn't play games with him."

"Says the girl who had two guys fighting over her." Cindy bumped her shoulder into Molly. "Some of us have to play the game if we want to win."

"Well, you're wrong. Mike likes you. Give him a chance." She giggled. "That's what you told me about Hayden. Take your own advice."

Cindy looked at Mike again and shrugged. "Maybe you're right." When he looked up and smiled at Cindy, she smiled back. The whistle blew, and Mike turned his head to focus on the game, but the smile stayed on his lips.

Molly nudged Cindy again. "See, you made his night. Now if they lose, he has something to look forward to."

Cindy snorted. "Nuh uh. If he loses, he's out." She cupped her hands again. "Let's go Tigers! Don't let them through, back line, or there'll be hell to pay!"

Molly laughed again. So did Mike on the field. When Altgeld's forward ran toward him, Mike dove in headfirst and grabbed the ball. He passed it to Hayden who took it toward Altgeld's side of the field.

"That's it, that's it! Nice job, keeper!'" Cindy yelled. Molly didn't see Mike's reaction. She kept her focus on Hayden while he dodged the other team, wincing when he took another elbow to the gut from the defender. He passed the ball to John on the far side of the field and then ran toward the goal.

"Damn he's fast." Cindy whistled. "Can't wait for track season."

Molly squeezed her fists and bounced on her toes. Hayden continued toward the goal. John tried to pass back to Hayden but didn't kick it far enough. Altgeld regained control of the ball, and the students in the stands groaned.

Molly sighed. "They're playing better, but Altgeld is just too good. And they're double-teaming Hayden when he gets the ball. He can't get anywhere."

Cindy shook her head. "I wish Tim was here. It'd be a whole new game."

A voice from behind shot through Molly's chest like a spear. "Yeah, too bad he's in juvie because of you, Molly."

Molly turned to face Andrea. She must have snuck up behind them after the second half started. Molly shook her head and turned away. She wouldn't get into it with Andrea tonight.

"If we lose it's your fault. You're the one who caused the trouble."

Molly grabbed Cindy's arm. "Ignore her. She's not worth it."

"She best keep her trap shut. I have nothing to lose now. I'll kick her ass worse than before."

A few students snickered at Cindy's threat. Andrea said nothing.

On the field, Altgeld had the ball. Mike came out of his box and saved a sure goal. He slid in on the rushing forward and hit the ball away. The guy fell to the ground, the ball rebounding off his feet and going out of bounds. Altgeld's fans screamed for a yellow card. The ref waved his hands and signaled a goal kick.

"That was a clean tackle. Nothing but ball." Cindy glared at the opposing team's fans.

Molly stared at Cindy with one brow raised. "How do you know so much about soccer?" She knew the game from watching with Trevor, but Cindy had never come with them.

Cindy grinned. "I played soccer until I was twelve. Then I decided I liked running better. I guess I never told you."

Molly laughed. "See, you and Mike have something in common. You can talk soccer moves on your first date."

Cindy gazed at Mike again. "He is cute, isn't he?" She stared for a moment with a smile on her face. She looked sideways at Molly and her smile turned to a smirk. "What the hell. I'll give it a shot."

"Good, we can double date sometime. That will be fun."

Cindy nodded. "Yeah, but don't you dare tell my mom. She'd skin him alive if she found out."

Molly nodded. Cindy's mom was scary.

Mike kicked the ball back into play and the game resumed. This time the Tigers had the ball. Hayden passed to the opposite side of the field and once again ran toward the goal. About halfway there he slowed, two defenders keeping pace with him, knocking him around with their bodies. Hayden called out, "Now, now, now!"

Cindy frowned. "Why is he calling for the ball? He's covered."

While Hayden battled to get away from the defenders, John ran up the side of the field.

Cindy put her hands on the sides of her head. "Where the hell is he going, he's a holding mid. He's out of position."

Altgeld's forward made a run for the Tiger goal and with nobody in the midfield to stop him he had a free shot toward the back corner. Molly held her breath and looked at the play clock. One minute remained. If Altgeld scored now, there was no time to recover.

John still ran up the line. Hayden tried to get away from the defenders, pushing them back with his hands and trying to run around them.

Mike moved away from the goal to midfield and screamed for the ball. The left-back passed it to him and he blasted the ball toward the sideline. John received the ball and ran. With Altgeld's right-back helping to guard Hayden, nobody was there to oppose John. Before Altgeld could stop it, John hit the ball. It slid past the near post and into the goal. The crowd screamed.

Hayden was the first one to reach John. He grabbed him around the waist and lifted him up, then the rest of the team piled on top in a heap. Molly and Cindy screamed with the rest of the student section. Everyone hugged and jumped together.

"Tigers! Tigers!" Cindy cheered, and everyone took up the words.

On the field, the team ran back to their positions. Ten seconds remained on the clock and Altgeld had to kick off. They made one last ditch effort to kick it in from mid field, but the ball landed short and the timer went off.

Everyone celebrated again. She smiled as Hayden and his team walked around the field to slap hands with the dejected Altgeld players, and then returned to the bench to celebrate.

"I can't believe it. This is awesome!" She smiled at Hayden. Tomorrow was her turn. The feeling of rightness settled over her again. "Come on, Cindy. Let's go wait for the guys."

Molly pulled Cindy toward the stairs. They tried to weave through the craziness of everyone celebrating. She was near the aisle when someone pushed her from behind.

Molly fell, throwing out her hands to catch herself. One arm smashed into the bleacher seat and pain shot up her arm. Then her head hit the same seat with the force of a sledgehammer.

"Molly are you okay?" Cindy touched her shoulder. A couple people laughed and someone else shushed them.

Molly sat up and blinked. Her head spun, and her arm hurt. "What the hell?" she asked. "I think someone pushed me."

She stood up and wobbled. She blinked her eyes to clear them, but someone pounded on her head from the inside, shaking her eyes. She raised her hand to the lump just under her hair behind her right ear.

Cindy looked around. "Who pushed you?"

Molly glanced around but had trouble focusing on the faces. "I don't know." She rubbed her sore arm and circled her wrist, wincing. "Come on, let's go."

From the next row up, Andrea smirked at her. Molly narrowed her eyes.

Andrea looked away and laughed.

Molly shook her head. Maybe their family could get a group discount on anger management classes. She and Cindy walked to the side of the field to wait.

"You okay, Molly? You don't look good." Cindy frowned and touched her cheek.

"I'll be fine. I can't believe I fell." She didn't want to tell Cindy she had a huge bump on her head. She'd freak out and probably make her go to the ER.

"Are you hurt?" Cindy pointed a finger at Molly. "You have to run tomorrow. If you're hurt, don't lie."

Molly rolled her eyes and leaned on the fence to cover her unsteadiness. "I'm fine. My arm hurts, but it's nothing."

Cindy grabbed Molly's arm. "Does this hurt?" Cindy gently squeezed Molly's wrist.

Molly winced but shook her head. "Not that much. I think I bruised it." She looked up when the students cheered again. The team headed off the field and ran toward the fence where Molly and Cindy stood.

Hayden spotted her and smiled. She smiled back, trying to hide her pain.

"Hey, we did it!" Hayden grabbed her around the waist and spun. Molly buried her head in his shoulder to keep from getting dizzy. He set her feet on the ground and kissed her.

"Congratulations." She smiled, but tears blurred her vision. She had a hard time focusing on Hayden's face and her heart raced. Something was wrong, something bad.

Hayden touched her cheek. "Are you okay?" He examined her eyes and frowned.

Molly kissed him again to buy time. "I'm just happy for you. These are happy tears, idiot."

Hayden studied her. "I have to go to the locker room. We'll talk more when I come back. Don't go anywhere." He kissed her, and then grabbed Mike's arm and pulled him away from Cindy. They followed the team toward the locker room.

After he walked away, Molly rubbed her head. Cindy smiled looking after Mike. Her smile faded when she turned to Molly. "What is wrong? And don't tell me nothing. You look like you're about to pass out."

Molly groaned and sat on the ground, holding her stomach. "I hit my head when I fell and now, I have a horrible headache." Nausea crept in to join the pain in her head.

Cindy joined her, worry plain on her face. "You need to go to the doctor."

Molly shook her head. "No, I'll be okay. Tylenol will help."
If she could keep it down.

Cindy reached into her purse. She pulled out a small pill
container and produced two painkillers. "Here, I always carry
ibuprofen." She handed them to Molly.

"I need water. Let's go to the concession stand." She stood
and wobbled again on her feet. Her fear overtook her desire to
pretend she was okay. "Damn it, Cindy. What am I going to do?
What if I can't run tomorrow?"

Cindy hugged her. Molly leaned on her for support. "You'll
be fine, Molly. You need to go rest and tomorrow things will be
better." Cindy held Molly's arm and led her toward a water fountain.
"Take the pills."

Molly put the pills in her mouth and leaned to drink. She
stood and lost her balance, wobbling again. Tears spilled onto her
cheeks and she wiped them away.

Cindy held Molly's arm. "Let's sit and wait for Hayden. He
can take you home."

"No, he'll want to celebrate with the team. I don't want to go home yet. If I sit here for a few minutes, I'll feel better. Don't tell him I got hurt. I don't want him to worry."

Cindy nodded. They waited in silence for the guys to return. The nausea passed, and Molly felt slightly better.

Hayden and Mike came out of the locker room, hair damp from showering. Molly and Cindy stood. At least Molly didn't wobble anymore. The ibuprofen had helped.

Hayden studied her while he approached. He returned her smile and kissed her. "Now, tell me what's wrong."

She leaned into his hand and closed her eyes. "Nothing is wrong. Let's go celebrate." She grinned. "I have a curfew tonight because I have to get up early. Big day tomorrow you know."

Hayden shook his head. "Yes, I know. I also know you're lying." He reached up to touch her hair. His fingers brushed the bump on her head, and she yelped.

Hayden's eyes widened, and he gently felt the lump. "Molly, what the hell happened? Why do you have a gigantic bump on your head?"

Cindy glared at her. "You didn't tell me that. Now I know you're going to the doctor."

Mike raised his eyebrows. "What happened to Molly?"

"Someone pushed her in the bleachers, and she fell and hit her head. She told me she had a headache but didn't tell me she had a bump. I'm taking her to the hospital."

Hayden nodded. "I'll drive."

Molly glared at Cindy then Hayden. "No, I'm not going to the hospital. Everyone calm down and stop freaking out."

Hayden glared back at her. "You need to get checked out. What if you have a concussion? You can't just go home and go to sleep." The glare disappeared, and fear took its place. "Please, just let us take you."

Molly sighed. "I want to go home." She laid her head on Hayden's chest. He wrapped his arms around her, strong and warm. She leaned into him.

"Fine but I'm not leaving you alone. I'm sure your mom would understand. Let's go."

Molly turned to Cindy and Mike. "Sorry, guess you'll have to celebrate without us." She hugged Cindy and whispered in her ear. "Have fun. Your first date should be alone, anyway."

Cindy snorted. "Feel better. I'll see you tomorrow when you win the race."

Molly smiled. "Don't jinx me. But thanks."

Hayden shook hands with Mike. "Don't celebrate too hard. Tell everyone I'll see them later."

Mike nodded and took Cindy's hand. "Later, Hayden. I hope you feel better, Molly. Good luck tomorrow, too."

"Thanks, Mike." Molly and Cindy exchanged a smile, then Cindy walked away with Mike.

She turned to Hayden and frowned. "You can take me home then go be with the team. You shouldn't miss the fun because of me."

He touched her chin and rubbed his fingers on her neck. "You're more important than a party." He took her hand and pulled her toward his car.

At her house, Hayden called his parents and waited in the kitchen while Molly changed into her pajamas. When she returned, he handed her an ice pack.

"Here. You need to bring the swelling down. It should help with your headache."

She held the ice to her head and sighed. "That feels good. Thanks."

Hayden led her to the couch. He sat and pulled her against his chest. "I'm staying here until your mom gets home. Sleep, but I'll wake you every half hour to check on you."

Molly sighed and held him tight. "Dr. Bishop. That has a nice ring to it. You sure you don't want to major in medicine instead of business?"

He chuckled and kissed her hair. "No, you'll be my only patient. Until I'm a dad and have to invest in Band-Aids."

Molly's stomach flipped, but not because of her injuries. "Having kids means we have to do something else first." She snuggled deeper into his arms. His heartbeat raced under her cheek.

"Well, seventeen is too young to think about marriage."

Molly lifted her head to see Hayden's face. "I wasn't talking about marriage."

He rolled his eyes. "Don't you know the old song? First comes love then comes marriage…" He grinned. "I think you have a one-track mind."

Molly smiled and laid her head back on Hayden.

He hugged her tighter. "I love you."

"I love you, too. Thanks for taking care of me." She closed her eyes and the weariness hit her. "I'll see you in half an hour. Unless you want to work on those private lessons."

"I can't believe I have to turn you down again. You know, you're making it hard to behave myself." He sighed. "Go to sleep." He picked up the ice pack and held it on her head.

"Thanks." She closed her eyes and drifted off to sleep with a smile on her face.

Hayden woke her a few times, but she barely kept her eyes open to answer his questions. The last time she woke, Hayden was placing her in her bed. She was too tired to get excited about it.

"Molly, your mom is home. I'm leaving but I'll see you in the morning." He kissed her, and she grabbed his shoulders.

She winced at the pain in her arm. "Stay with me."

She couldn't even open her eyes. Hayden's chuckle bounced around her head.

He took her hands and placed them on her chest then pulled the blankets up to her chin. At least she was sober this time he tucked her in bed.

"Good night, Molly."

"Good night, Hayden." She barely got the words out before she was asleep.

CHAPTER THIRTY-ONE

HAYDEN

When Hayden arrived the next morning. Molly greeted him in her kitchen with a hug.

"Hi." She grinned. "Thanks for tucking me in again last night. It's a good thing my mom was here. People will talk."

Hayden scanned her face for signs of pain. "How do you feel today?"

"Great. No more lump and my head feels better." She glanced at her mom. "My mom told me you explained everything to her last night."

Her mom laughed. "Yes, after I almost kicked Hayden in the face because I didn't know who he was sitting on the couch in the dark."

Molly giggled. "Mom, you can't fight an intruder."

Hayden raised an eyebrow. "I don't know, she had me scared. Your mom is tough." He looked at Molly's arm. "What's with the bandage?"

She touched the ace bandage wrapped around her wrist. She glanced between her mom and Hayden. "It's nothing. I noticed it felt stiff this morning and I thought I should wrap it." She stepped away and went to the refrigerator. "Did you eat? We have cereal if you want."

Hayden and Lisa exchanged a look.

Lisa grabbed her jacket. "I'll go start the car. Sometimes it's stubborn."

Hayden jingled his keys. "I can drive."

Lisa shook her head. "Nope, this is my parental badge of honor. I get to drive my baby girl to her final state competition."

Her mom walked out and Molly grinned. "She's emotional today. Hungry?"

Hayden shook his head. "I already ate. Are you sure you feel back to normal?"

She groaned. "I'm fine. I'm nervous about the race so please stop asking about my health." She carried her empty bowl to the sink.

"Okay, I'll wait until after you win the race and have your offer from UCLA in your hand."

"Please, tell me you applied there, too."

Hayden waved his hand. "Sure."

Molly's smile grew. "So, you've already got an acceptance?"

Hayden wrinkled his nose looked at the floor. "Actually, I only applied last week, when you told me they were interested in you."

Molly put her arms around his neck. He held her waist and swallowed hard, reminding himself Lisa could walk in any second.

"No matter what happens today, I only want to be with you." Molly met his gaze, hers filled with the determined fire he loves so much. "If we end up at different schools, my feelings for you won't change."

His hands trembled on her hips. "I know. But I hope we are at the same school. I don't want be away from you."

She hugged him, and he squeezed his eyes shut. He'd never felt so emotional before Molly. Now he cried like a little old man remembering his dead war buddies. Love was hard.

Lisa walked in and stopped inside the doorway. Molly let go of Hayden and he stepped back. Lisa smiled. "Sorry, I didn't mean to interrupt. It's time to go."

Molly grabbed her bag. Hayden took it from her and carried it to the car. During the hour-long drive to the course, they listened to the radio. Molly played DJ while Hayden rode in the backseat, singing every song while Molly and Lisa laughed.

They pulled into the parking lot at the meet and Hayden took a deep breath. This was it, Molly's big chance. "Are you ready?" He touched her shoulder.

She reached up with her good hand and held his. "I'm ready."

Lisa parked, and they got out of the car. Lisa scanned the busy field. "Where do you need to go?"

"I have to meet the coach at the team tent. Keep an eye out for Cindy. She's supposed to be here too." Molly hugged her mom. Lisa's eyes filled with tears again. "Mom stop it. This is a happy day."

Lisa sniffed and wiped her eyes. "Sorry, it's just I can't believe you're growing up so fast. This is your last race in high school."

"Yes, but, Mom, after this you can watch me run for my college team."

"I know, but it won't be the same. Then you'll be a woman in college and not my little girl."

Molly laughed. "She would get along great with your mom, Hayden."

He nodded. "They could compare our baby books."

Lisa smirked at them. "All right, I get the picture. I'll try not to cry anymore if you promise to run your best."

"Deal." Molly hugged her again.

"I need to find a rest room. Good luck, Molly. Hayden, I'll meet you back here in a few minutes."

She walked away, and Molly smiled. "She knows we wanted to be alone for a minute."

"Your mom is great. Let's not waste the time she gave us." He pulled her into his arms and kissed her like she had kissed him on the couch in his basement. Hayden rubbed her back for a moment then released her.

Molly drew a deep shaky breath. He could see his desire mirrored in her silver eyes. He touched her bottom lip with his finger. "If you want to finish that kiss you have to run for it. I'll be waiting at the finish line."

She swallowed. "That's mean."

"Only if you don't show up."

She laughed. "I'll be there. We may need to wait until we're alone though. One more kiss like that and I can't be held responsible for my actions." She tapped his nose with her finger. "I have to go. Wish me luck."

Hayden hugged her. "You don't need luck when you have skill. Now go run your race."

"Thanks." She squeezed his hand and left for the tent. Hayden frowned.

Lisa walked up beside him, her gaze on Molly's retreating back. "I'm scared, Hayden. When she woke up, she looked like death warmed over. She's holding it together, but just barely."

Hayden nodded. "She's stubborn. She wouldn't let us take her to the ER last night. We wanted to, Lisa." Hayden wished he and Cindy had forced Molly to go.

Lisa placed her hand on Hayden's arm. "She's very stubborn. Let's hope she can use that in the race today."

"If you don't mind, I'd like to run around alone and keep track of her today."

Lisa smiled. "I'll wait here at the finish for her."

They waited for Cindy by the concession stand. When she showed up with Mike, Hayden smiled. He shook Mike's hand. "Hey, Mike. Never thought I'd see you at a meet."

"Me either." Mike glanced at Cindy.

Cindy's eyebrows traveled up her forehead. "And what's that supposed to mean?"

Hayden nodded to Mike. "Mike's a one sport guy. He's all soccer." He looked at their joined hands. Hayden stepped back and waved to Mike. "Mike, this is Molly's mom, Lisa." Mike and Lisa shook hands.

"Nice to meet you, Mike." Lisa winked at Cindy. Cindy blushed.

"How's Molly today?" Cindy asked.

Hayden sighed. "She says she's better."

Cindy smirked. "Right, I know what that means. That girl's a stubborn fool. I hope she doesn't blow it today."

Lisa frowned. "We're trying to be positive."

Hayden touched her shoulder. "She'll be okay."

They went to the starting line area to wait for the teams and Hayden studied the course map until the teams lined up in the corrals.

Hayden looked for Molly, following her steps as she did her first warm-up run. Her face had the focused mask she usually wore. She looked healthy and strong.

"Here we go." Lisa's whispered words shook. She looked at him. "Keep an eye on her, Hayden."

He patted her shoulder. "I'll yell at her for you."

The announcer came on the loudspeaker and welcomed them to the state final. The sun shone and the trees surrounding the park sported leaves in full color. Perfect weather and a perfect location. Hayden prayed for a perfect race from Molly.

"Ladies, at the sound of the gun the race will begin. Good luck to all competitors. Please take your marks." The microphone cut off and the speaker crackled. Hayden swallowed his fear, his gaze focused on Molly at the start line.

She stared at the ground in front of her, unblinking, her hands hung ready by her sides. The bandage on her arm looked tighter, like she'd squeezed on a too-small sock. Hayden frowned, wondering if it hurt.

The gun cracked, and he jumped. Molly bolted away from the other girls. Only a handful kept up with her.

Cindy gave her analysis. "She looks good. Nice controlled start. She's going out fast to gain ground on them. That way she doesn't get caught up in the massive pack."

"I'll be back." Hayden ran away to meet Molly at the half mile mark. The pace truck went by and he watched for her. She was in the lead with three other girls close behind her. Her gaze was focused on the trail, her arms moved loosely at her sides, relaxed.

"That's it, Molly. Keep your pace!"

Molly didn't acknowledge his yell. Her arms swung easily. Her legs flashed in the sunlight filtering between the leaves above.

Hayden smiled. She looked normal, strong and healthy—and ready to kick ass. He turned and ran to the mile and a half marker. It was close, so he got there before the truck this time.

When it arrived, Hayden's chest tightened. Molly had lost the lead and fallen to second place. In the short time since he'd seen her, her condition deteriorated. Her sweat-soaked face was pale. She still pumped her legs and swung her arms, but instead of her smooth gate, it looked like she was trying hard to keep up with the girl in front of her.

"Come on Molly. Dig deep. You can still catch her." He glared at the slight shake of her head. She wouldn't give up. Not if he could help it.

"Don't give me that look. Dig!" She grinned. He hoped his admonition would be enough to push her.

After she passed, Hayden sprinted to the finish. He bounced from foot to foot, waiting for the pace truck to come into view. Molly had closed the gap on the leader. They raced around the curve, and then it was a full out sprint to the finish across a grassy field. The crowd screamed, pushing the girls forward.

Hayden looked at Molly's face and his chest constricted. Ghostly white and eyes with a glassy spaced-out look, she slowed, and the gap increased.

"Come on, Molly. You're almost there. Push to the finish!" She might not even make it. The winner crossed the line and the crowd cheered for her. Molly was behind her by a few seconds but stumbled across the finish line in second place. She collapsed to the ground, unmoving. The screams of the crowd stopped, replaced with gasps of concern.

Hayden stared at Molly's limp form laying on the ground, his heart in his throat, his mouth opened in shock. He ran toward the finish line. The trainers were there when he came around the barricade.

"You can't go in there, son." An official held him back.

Lisa appeared at Hayden's side. "That's my daughter."

The man held her back, too. "The trainers have it under control. Go to the Med tent over there. They'll bring her there in a minute." He pointed to a tent behind them. Hayden took Lisa's arm. Cindy stood behind her, tears streaming on her cheeks and Mike's arm around her shoulders.

"Come on. Let's go wait for her." Hayden pulled Lisa and she nodded.

When Molly got to the tent, she was awake, but groggy. Lisa hugged her, crying again. "Are you okay? You scared me half to death."

"I'm okay, Mom." She rubbed her head. "I didn't win, did I?"

Lisa stepped aside. Hayden hugged Molly next.

"You got second." He trembled when she hugged him back. "God, Molly. You scared me, too." He knew he should let go, but he couldn't. He held her tight to his chest his own eyes filling fast.

Cindy tapped him on the shoulder. "Hey, you had your turn, now move it."

Hayden wiped his eyes. Cindy surprised Hayden by hugging him, not Molly.

"She's okay. Don't let her see you cry. You'll upset her."

He nodded.

Cindy hugged Molly, turning her away so Hayden could get it together before Molly saw how upset he was.

Mike pursed his lips and whistled. "She's tough. I've never seen anything like that. No wonder you're crazy obsessed with her." He smiled, and Hayden chuckled.

The doctor approached with Molly's coach. "I'm Dr. Standfill." He shook Lisa's hand. "It seems this girl has a concussion. Any idea how?"

They explained the fall at the soccer game. When Cindy told them about Molly's arm, the doctor frowned. "Can I remove that bandage, Molly?"

She nodded and looked at the ground as the doctor removed the bandage.

Hayden gasped at the purple bruise covering Molly's arm. He lifted her chin with his finger, forcing her to meet his eyes.

"You have a broken arm." He glared at her. "The next time we say you're going to the ER, we're tying you up and forcing you to go."

Cindy glared, too. "I'll bring the rope."

The doctor laughed. "Well, young lady. It sounds like you won't get away with this again." He shook his head. "I've never seen someone concussed with an unset broken arm get second place at the state finals. You may not have set a record time, but you're the first to do that."

He reached for his bag. After setting her arm in a splint he patted her knee. "Be sure to get this checked out when you get home. You're tough. I can't wait to see you run in college. Good luck." He walked away smiling and shaking his head. Lisa and the coach followed.

Molly hung her head, tears falling in her lap. "I'm sorry I made you all worry. And I'm sorry I didn't win."

Hayden sat on the cot next to her. She wrapped her arms around his neck and sobbed. He held her and rubbed her back. "We don't care if you didn't win. You did your best. If you hadn't gotten hurt, it would have been a piece of cake. To get second the way you did, they way you felt, that's what winners do. You didn't quit."

Her sobs slowed and turned to hiccups.

Cindy took Mike's hand. "We'll go get some water."

Hayden rubbed Molly's hair, whispering in her ear. "I love you, Molly. Please don't scare me like that again."

She leaned back to look at him and Hayden caught his breath. Her eyes were puffy, and her hair was a mess, but even in her pain, she was the most beautiful thing he'd ever seen. He saw forever in that beauty.

"I think you owe me something." She grinned. "I crossed the finish line. I want the rest of that kiss now."

Hayden huffed a laugh. "I thought you wanted to wait until we were alone."

She shrugged. "Well, how about a normal kiss then." She pulled him to her. He reached up to touch her cheek and wiped away the wetness from her tears, kissing her softly.

"Get a room."

Hayden laughed at Mike as they walked back into the tent. "Jealous? Nobody asked you to watch. You have someone to distract you now." He winked at Cindy and Molly laughed.

Cindy sniffed and raised her chin. "Whatever, Hayden. I have more class than to make out in the med tent at state. Just because you…"

Mike grabbed Cindy and kissed her. She reached up and held his face, pulling him back when he tried to stop.

Hayden laughed again

Molly shook her head. "That's the second time in my life I've seen Cindy speechless. Anybody notice the quiet?"

Cindy let go of Mike and narrowed her eyes at Molly. "Don't think just because you're injured, I won't whoop your ass for disrespecting me. I'll…"

Molly laughed. "Moo, moo."

Cindy held her breath then burst into laughter.

Hayden raised his eyebrows at Mike and the girls laughed harder. They stopped when coach Davis and Lisa approached.

Lisa glanced at them all. "Molly, Coach Davis wants to talk to you."

Hayden stood to leave, and Molly grabbed his hand. "You all can stay." She frowned. "I think I know what you're going to say, Coach. I didn't get the scholarship, did I?"

The coach gave her a sad smile. "UCLA passed. Your time was five seconds off the other girl they were eyeing. They didn't even wait to see what happened. Once you crossed the line they left."

Hayden put his arm around Molly. She rubbed her head and leaned against him. He squeezed her shoulders. "I'm so sorry. It's their loss."

She nodded. "Yeah, but it's mine too." She wiped her eyes with her uninjured hand.

The coach cleared her throat. "Molly, that's a tough blow. You worked so hard this year. I have good news though."

The coach waved to someone. Hayden recognized him. The scout from U of I.

He shook Molly's hand. "Hi, Molly, nice to see you again."

"Hello, Coach Tompkins. Are you here to tell me I didn't get your scholarship either?" Molly sniffled.

"I've never seen a runner do what you did today, Molly." He chuckled and shook his head. "I don't recommend running injured, but what you did took heart. That's the type of runner I want on my team." He glanced at Lisa then back to Molly. "I'm prepared to give you a full ride for four years at U of I. If you want it, we'd love to have a runner like you join us."

Molly blinked, she turned to her mom's smiling tear-streaked face. She looked at Hayden's grin then back to the coach. "Tell me one thing first."

Coach Tompkins raised his brows. "What do you need to know?"

Molly narrowed her eyes, silver flashing in the dark tent. "Do you have a meet with UCLA scheduled for next season?"

The coach lifted his chin and smiled. "We do."

She nodded. "Then I accept your offer."

Hayden laughed, and Lisa cried. Cindy screamed and jumped around the tent until Mike grabbed her and she hugged him.

"Welcome to the fighting Ilini, Molly. I'll see you in the spring on signing day." He winked. "Get that head and arm healed up. UCLA won't know what hit them."

Molly smirked. "You're right, they won't."

He nodded then walked away with Molly's coach.

Lisa hugged her. "I'm so proud of you, Molly."

"Thanks, Mom."

"I'll go get the car. You and Hayden come out by the main entrance in ten minutes and I'll pick you up. Then we are taking you to the hospital." She patted Molly's head before she left.

Molly glanced at Cindy. "Would you mind getting my bag from the team tent?"

"Sure, then I can go brag on you to the others. That way it gets back to Andrea." Cindy snorted. "You know she's the one who pushed you last night."

Mike frowned. "She's never invited to my parties again." He shook his head and Cindy pulled him out of the tent.

"That will seriously cut into her beer supply. Maybe she'll run better next year." Hayden sat next to her on the cot again. "Good thing Mike didn't cut her off this year."

"True." Molly's smile faded. "Hayden, can I ask you something?" Molly met his eyes with a serious gaze. She touched her temple with her uninjured hand.

Hayden frowned. "What is it? Is your head hurting again? Do you need something?"

She reached over and held his face. "Please." Her whisper was rough.

"What?" Hayden waited, his gaze bouncing around her face.

"Please, tell me you applied to U of I."

Hayden laughed. He pulled her into his arms and gave her the rest of his kiss. Panting, he stopped and leaned his forehead against hers. "I did *and* I have my acceptance letter." He laughed at her tears and kissed her again.

Molly wiped her eyes. "Thank, God. But, do you know what the best part is?"

Hayden shrugged. "No, what's that?"

She looked around the med tent and smiled a devious smile, leaning in to whisper in his ear. "My scholarship includes a private room."

Hayden grinned and whispered back to Molly. "That's good, but I don't think I can wait that long."

"It's not that long. And besides, we have forever you know."

Hayden pulled her into his arms and sang. "First comes love, then comes marriage, then comes Molly with the…"

"Shut up you idiot and kiss me."

And he did. The first kiss of forever.

****

AUTHOR'S NOTE

Thank you so much for reading Breaking the Bro Code. This book was a labor of love, not to mention, lots of late nights and caffeine. If you enjoyed it, please spread the word with others who may also like to read about Hayden and Molly. Also, please leave a **review** to let other readers know how much you enjoyed the story. You can find more information about my other books on my web page and my social media contacts are listed below. I would love to hear from you, so please leave me a message.

Happy reading!

B.B. Swann

Website: https://www.bbswann.com/

Twitter: https://twitter.com/BB_Swann

Facebook: https://www.facebook.com/BBSWANN/

Instagram: https://www.instagram.com/bunnie93s/

If you, or someone you know is in an abusive relationship, there is someone who wants to help. Go to the National Domestic Violence Hotline for more information.

ABOUT THE AUTHOR

B.B. Swann wanted to be a writer when she realized writing words was easier than saying them out loud. Still, somehow, she became a teacher and talks quite a bit.

B.B. Swann lives in Southern Illinois with her two- and four-legged family members. She loves to run, binge watch Netflix health documentaries, and talk to her three grown children when they have a minute to spare.

Most nights you can find her reading or writing into the wee hours of the night. She believes in the almighty power of caffeine and battling old age with purple hair and lots of sarcasm.

OTHER BOOKS BY BB SWANN

BREAKING THE BARRIERS -(8/20/19) Stay in the 80's and read book 2 about the story of Mike and Cindy!

BREAKING THE CYCLE-(9/1/2020)

3rd and final book in the 80s series about Andrea and Gio!

KATIE COMMA- (PB) The teacher opens a window and Katie Comma is blown from her book! She dodges the curious children, diving into their books to hide. But the sentences aren't afraid to tell her she's in the wrong place. Alone and scared, Katie perseveres, determined to find the place where a lost comma belongs. (Pelican Publishing Company; Illust. by Maja Andersen)

TWISTED FAIRY TALES- by Aeon Writers: a short story anthology of scifi and fantasy-based fairy tale inspired stories.

SNEAK PEEK

BREAKING THE BARRIERS

CHAPTER ONE

Mike

Mike Ryan never wanted to be a stalker, but he sure rocked the job.

Glancing at Cindy Wilson across the classroom, he caught his breath. Maybe he should feel special. Lucky. Call Guinness. Not many guys had permission to spy on their own girlfriends. But damn, he felt like a creep following her around.

Hide their relationship at all costs. Nobody could know. Not that he cared, but she would. Aside from their best friends, Hayden and Molly, nobody else in their Elkwood High class of 1986 knew they were dating. And it totally sucked.

Mike tapped his pen against his notebook, one smack for each tick from the clock above the door. Five minutes. Five more minutes until their biology class ended, and he'd follow her—again. Looking back to the teacher as he droned on about DNA in his gravely pack-a-day voice, Mike leaned back in his chair. The molded blue plastic dug into his back and he sighed.

Cindy turned her head at the noise, making eye contact, but ended it before he could react.

Three minutes. Tap. Tap. Tap.

Two minutes. Tap. Tap.

She brushed a stray hair from her face and Mike flexed his fingers. He forced his gaze back to the teacher.

"Don't forget," their teacher said, "your third quarter project outline is due tomorrow."

The last ear-splitting bell rang, and everyone talked at once. Chairs scraped and sneakers squeaked against the tiled floor. Two guys squeezed past Mike, bumping into him on their way to the door, racing toward freedom.

Mike gathered his books, peeking again at Cindy from the corner of his eye. She laughed at something Molly said and he clenched his jaw.

Melissa, a girl he'd dated a few times last year, patted his arm. "Later, Mike."

He smiled, sparing her a glance. "Yeah, see ya."

He turned his head back in time to catch Cindy's glare. She shoved a book into her bag and stomped out the door. Grinning at her reaction, he followed.

It had been so long since he'd been on an official date, even his self-absorbed mother asked him why he never went anywhere. It was bogus concern. She only noticed because she had to stay home when his dad nixed her requests for the two of them to *get away*—again. He wished his dad would take her somewhere, so she'd leave him alone about his lack of a social life.

Mike weaved through the crowded hall, his gaze focused on Cindy's athletic form gliding between the big-haired girls with their padded shoulders. Cindy stood out in a crowd, and not because she was the only black girl in their small, Illinois town. Her don't-mess-with-me attitude and talents on the track made her special.

She stopped at her locker and Mike slipped to the opposite side of the hall to take a drink from the water fountain. A pair of white Keds appeared next to his feet, smooth-skinned legs starting inside the sneaker and extending past his view.

"I've been looking for you, Mike."

He muffled a groan, wiping his mouth with the back of his hand and standing to face she shoe owner. To his left stood Jenny, a junior from his trig class. Across the hall, Cindy met his eyes and frowned.

Jenny walked her fingers up the sleeve of his jean jacket. "A few of us are going for frozen yogurt. Want to go?"

She flashed her dimples, flipping her long blonde hair. She liked to point out that it was the same shade as his whenever she badgered him for a date. As if matching hair meant they should be together—like Barbie and Ken.

The echo of metal on metal hit his ears as Cindy slammed her locker.

"Sorry, got plans." He bit back a smile and moved his arm from Jenny's reach to scratch a fake itch on his head.

"Are you sure?" She leaned closer and put both her hands on his chest. A cloud of perfume encircled his head and his eyes watered. "If you keep telling me no, I'll think you don't like me."

He opened his mouth as Cindy bumped into Jenny's side, knocking her away from him.

She smirked at Jenny. "Oops, sorry. Got pushed. Crossing the hall is like playing Frogger."

"Right." Jenny rubbed her shoulder.

Cindy stepped between them and shot a wide-eyed glance at Mike before bending to get a drink from the fountain, her hip touching his leg.

Trying to ignore the heat from her touch, he shook his head at Jenny. "I have to be somewhere after school."

Cindy stepped back from the water fountain and bumped again into Jenny. "Excuse me,"

Jenny turned her back to Cindy and smiled at him. "Okay. Maybe next time." She slid a hand up his arm and Cindy's eyes widened again.

"See ya later," Jenny said with a tap of her finger on his nose.

Mike smirked as Jenny brushed past Cindy, chin raised, and eyes narrowed.

Cindy glared back then turned her gaze to him.

He gave her a small grin.

"Hmph," she said, and strode toward the door.

He chuckled. At least her reaction meant she still liked him. The fun ended as they walked through the parking lot. For all the attention she gave him, the twenty feet between them could have been fifty miles. She didn't make eye contact, didn't look in his direction, didn't flip him off. Nothing. Just like every other day.

Sunlight reflected off the cars in the dusty gravel parking lot, and Mike squinted against the glare. Unlocking his red Camaro, he tossed his backpack in the back seat and glanced once more in her direction. His blood heated just thinking about touching her. Shiny black hair pulled into a curly ponytail, smooth caramel skin glowing in the sunshine—he'd memorized the softness during their hidden interactions.

Sucking in a breath of cold spring air, he hopped into the driver's seat and revved his engine, *Obsession* blasted from the speakers he'd left up too loud.

"Tell me something I don't know," he said to the radio. He sang along while he drove, following her blue Escort to the running trail outside of town—like Mario following Princess Peach.

Pulling into the lot right behind her, he parked next to her and cut the engine. With a blast of cool air, Cindy opened the door and slid into the passenger seat. Her sweet scent enveloped him, and he was home.

"Hey." She leaned toward him.

"Come here. I've waited all day for this." He held her face and kissed her, long and deep. He touched her shoulders, sliding his hands from her arms onto her waist. He pulled her closer, and she sighed.

She played with the spikes on top of his head while her lips moved softly against his.

When he finally let her go, her brown eyes twinkled in the sunlight streaming through the windshield. "How was your day?" she asked.

"Lonely." God, he sounded pathetic, but each day got harder and harder.

"Well, you had company after bio." She pressed her lips against his again.

He pulled away shaking his head. "Just ignore her. I do."

"She'd better keep her hands to herself." She touched his leg and heat raced across his thigh. "Next time I won't be so nice."

"Don't worry. It's not her hands I want touching me."

She caressed his cheek. "Come on. It's a nice day. Let's take a walk before I have to meet the others."

Mike's stomach tightened. Great. Another walk in the woods. Their relationship turned into a freaking fairy tale. Snow White and Prince Charming, kissing in the trees.

He held her hand, walking the ten feet to the trail head and stepping onto the uneven path. The leafless trees allowed the sun to reach them, making the cool breeze more bearable. A couple large branches from a broken maple tree hung across the trail. Jumping in front of Cindy, Mike held it back and wiped away the spider webs stretching between them. She passed through with a smile and took his offered hand again.

After a few minutes of listening to the conversations of the birds, they walked toward a large flat boulder set back under the trees. His white converse sank into the squishy leaves of last summer, sending he smell of wet earth up from the ground. They sat on the rock. Wrapping both arms around her, he pulled Cindy into his warmth.

She relaxed against him. "Are you excited about joining track?"

"Yes," he chuckled. "I can't believe I let you talk me into that. Senior year, most people drop out of sports, they don't join a new one." Mostly he looked forward to not having to miss out on time with her because she had practice. Not that he'd tell her that. He sounded pathetic enough without letting her know how obsessed he was with her.

"You'll do fine."

"Why do the girls start practicing before the guys?" He glanced around at the woods. They only met here so she'd be able to make it to practice on time on the other side of the park.

"Because," she said, straightening the lapel of his jacket. "We have a shot at going to state with our relays this year. We want to be conditioned. The more we run, the better we'll be."

"I hope you don't hold me to that standard. I've never even been to a meet. I might make an ass out of myself and get smoked on the track."

She raised her eyebrows and tucked in her chin. "You better not. I don't date guys who suck at sports."

"Keep up that attitude and I'll lose on purpose."

"That is the most ignorant thing you've ever said." She giggled as he tickled her. "Take it back."

"Only if you promise not to laugh at me tomorrow when I drop the ball on my foot."

"It's called a shot, and no way. I claim laughing rights anytime you do something *that* stupid."

"You're mean." He rested his cheek on the top of her head. "Maybe I should go home and practice. Want to come and help me?"

"I have to practice."

"How about afterward. Please?" He held his breath waiting for her answer.

Her shoulders stiffened. "I can't. You know that."

"I know you *think* that." He held her by the shoulders. "Nobody's there. We'll be alone."

"I want to.' Cindy frowned and dropped her gaze to the ground. 'But, I can't."

He blew out a frustrated breath. "No, you *won't*. There's a difference."

His body ached to sit with her on a couch, watch TV, listen to music, anything but walk in the trees or kiss in his car. As romantic as it should sound, it wasn't.

"I don't like this either." She pushed off the rock and sloshed through the muck back to the trail.

Mike pursed his lips, staring at her back, then jogged to her side. "The only thing stopping us from telling everyone we're dating is you." He gently grabbed her shoulder and turned her toward him.

"Do we have to argue again?"

"No," he said with a shaky grin. "You can just agree with me and then we can act like a real couple."

She gave a sarcastic laugh. "If I agree with you, then I won't be around to *be* a couple with you. My mom will kill me and feed me to the neighbors at a barbeque."

"C'mon, Cindy. She can't be that bad."

"When we moved here, Mama told me no dating until after high school. Her words were *Boys are nothing but trouble, and I'll whoop you into tomorrow if I catch you with one.* I don't want to cross, Mama."

Mike smirked. "When you moved here you were twelve. Maybe it's time to revisit that conversation."

"No, it's…" She glanced at her feet then over his shoulder. "It's not the right time."

"Is it your brother? Are you afraid of him telling your parents?" Chuckling, he stuck his hands in his pockets. "I mean don't you two have that weird twin bonding thing going on? You know, *Wonder Twin powers, activate.*"

"No," she said with a snort. "I can handle Elijah. That's not it."

Avoiding his eyes, she walked on toward the lot. Mike kicked a stone into the brush and followed. They reached their lonely cars in the sun-filled gravel lot.

He held her hands and pulled her toward him, staring into her eyes. Acceptance, belonging, passion, understanding, floated in their melted chocolate depths. He drew a shallow breath. It should be so easy. Why did she make it so hard?

"I want a real relationship, Cindy. Where we go on real dates and do real things together where everyone can see us and know we're together."

"You know I want the same things."

"Then let's *do* them." He held her hands to his chest. "If we both want things to change then why not change them?"

She stared back, biting her lip.

Is she really considering it this time? His heart jackhammered against his ribs.

Then Cindy shook her head, and his hopes landed in the dirt at his feet.

"We graduate in a few months. Once I'm at school and out of the house, we'll be free."

Months. More waiting. More hiding. More sacrifices from them both for reasons he didn't even understand. Maybe she didn't really share his feelings. Maybe she didn't like him as much as he did her. He bit his tongue and the taste of copper filled his mouth.

"Right. Let's keep hiding in the woods." He ignored her frown and walked to the Escort, pulling the door open. "Better get to practice, before you turn into a pumpkin."

"So, that's it?" She raised her eyebrows. "You don't want to hang out with me?"

"Of course I do. I always want to hang out with you. But not here." He glanced around at the trees, bare branches clacking in the wind, last year's nests visible without the leaves to hide them. Sad reminders of families long gone. He returned his gaze to hers, blinking against the sting in his eyes. "I can't do this anymore."

"You mean you *won't.* There's a difference," she mocked.

"I guess so."

"Fine. Then we won't." Cindy sniffled. She crossed her arms and turned to glare at the trees.

Staring at her profile, Mike swallowed the boulder from his throat. He'd gone too far this time. "Are you… are you breaking up with me?"

She gasped, whipping back around to face him. "What? No."

He lifted his gaze to hers, hands shaking at the rare tears that sparkled in her eyes. His stomach tightened and he ran a finger across her cheek.

She whispered, "Are you breaking up with *me*?"

Was he? Could he go back to meaningless dates with girls who didn't matter but would at least be seen in public with him? No, he could no sooner end this than he could solve a Rubik's cube without pulling off the stickers. But things had to change, or he'd go insane.

Cindy closed her eyes, and the tears slid down her face. "You are."

"I don't want to break up, but I can't keep hiding." Lifting his trembling hands, he wiped her tears away with his thumbs.

"Mike, what if… if people don't like us being together? There aren't any couples like us here."

"So? I don't care that your black and I'm white. It doesn't matter."

"To some people it will."

"Since when do you care what people think?"

"Since I have something they can ruin."

"You stand up to everyone who pisses you off or looks at you wrong. What makes this any different? Isn't this important enough to fight for?"

"Of course." She squeezed his hands. "But that's what scares me. People are assholes, Mike."

Mike leaned his forehead on hers. "If someone has a problem with us, they can deal with it."

"Yes, but…" The tremors in her bottom lip sent vibrations to his stomach.

"Let's start slow. Just tell our friends and the assholes at school. Your parents won't have to know, but everyone else will know how I feel for you." He forced a grin. "Then maybe Jenny will leave me alone."

She gave a soft laugh, tears spilling onto her cheeks.

"I promise," Mike said. "Just at school. I won't call your house or come to see you there or expect you to come to my house. Just… please."

This was it. His last argument. Slumping his shoulders, he swallowed back the bile rising in his throat. A no this time would send him over the edge.

Each thump of his pounding heart ticked away the longest ten seconds of his life. His chest constricted, sweat trickling down his back despite the coolness of the day. She shook her head, and the pounding changed to a stabbing pain.

But then she threw her arms around his neck. "You're right. I *do* want people to know." She pressed her face into his neck. "Okay, we'll start slow. Just at school."

He pulled her in for a kiss. "Thank you," he whispered on her lips.

She shook her head. "Thank me if we survive tomorrow. With the imminent stupidity of some of our classmates, you might change your mind."

"Nah. I can ignore them as long as you don't make me follow you around anymore."

A slow smile spread across her face. "I'll break the news to Jenny."

"Be gentle."

"Right." Cindy rolled her eyes. She kissed him on the cheek then laid her head on his chest. "I have to go. I'm gonna be late."

"Okay." He squeezed her then gestured to her open door. She got in and closed the door, her body rocking back and forth as she rolled down her window. Mike leaned through to give her one last kiss. "I'll see you tomorrow. I'll wait for you by the door."

"OK. See you at school." She touched his cheek then he stood back, waving as she drove away.

Driving home, relishing the warm feeling in his chest instead of the usual cold loneliness, he worried about Elijah's reaction to their relationship. Mike wasn't afraid of him, but he didn't want to have her brother mad at him. And he didn't want Elijah to nark on them to her parents.

He'd trust Cindy to take care of her brother and he'd focus on the others. This relationship would turn their little rural school upside down. But Mike would do whatever it took to be with her. How hard could it be?

Made in the USA
Middletown, DE
26 February 2020

85208963R00205